ELEVEN PIPERS PIPING

Twelve Days of Christmas

Emily E K Murdoch

ARE YOU SIGNED UP FOR DRAGONBLADE'S BLOG?

You'll get the latest news and information on exclusive giveaways, exclusive excerpts, coming releases, sales, free books, cover reveals and more.

Check out our complete list of authors, too!

No spam, no junk. That's a promise!

Sign Up Here

www.dragonbladepublishing.com

Dearest Reader;

Thank you for your support of a small press. At Dragonblade Publishing, we strive to bring you the highest quality Historical Romance from some of the best authors in the business. Without your support, there is no 'us', so we sincerely hope you adore these stories and find some new favorite authors along the way.

Happy Reading!

CEO, Dragonblade Publishing

Additional Dragonblade books by Author Emily E K Murdoch

Twelve Days of Christmas
Twelve Drummers Drumming
Eleven Pipers Piping
Ten Lords a Leaping
Nine Ladies Dancing

The De Petras Saga
The Misplaced Husband (Book 1)
The Impoverished Dowry (Book 2)
The Contrary Debutante (Book 3)
The Determined Mistress (Book 4)
The Convenient Engagement (Book 5)

The Governess Bureau Series
A Governess of Great Talents (Book 1)
A Governess of Discretion (Book 2)
A Governess of Many Languages (Book 3)
A Governess of Prodigious Skill (Book 4)
A Governess of Unusual Experience (Book 5)
A Governess of Wise Years (Book 6)
A Governess of No Fear (Novella)

Never The Bride Series
Always the Bridesmaid (Book 1)
Always the Chaperone (Book 2)
Always the Courtesan (Book 3)
Always the Best Friend (Book 4)
Always the Wallflower (Book 5)
Always the Bluestocking (Book 6)
Always the Rival (Book 7)
Always the Matchmaker (Book 8)

Always the Widow (Book 9)
Always the Rebel (Book 10)
Always the Mistress (Book 11)
Always the Second Choice (Book 12)
Always the Mistletoe (Novella)
Always the Reverend (Novella)

The Lyon's Den Connected World
Always the Lyon Tamer

Pirates of Britannia Series
Always the High Seas

De Wolfe Pack: The Series
Whirlwind with a Wolfe

Dear reader,

I adore Christmas, and I've chosen to include a few Christmas traditions in this story that embellishes the timeline. Though I haven't kept 100% to the historical record, I've chosen to do this to surround you with yuletide galore, so you can fall in love with my heroes and heroines in a glorious Christmas setting,

Enjoy!
Emily x

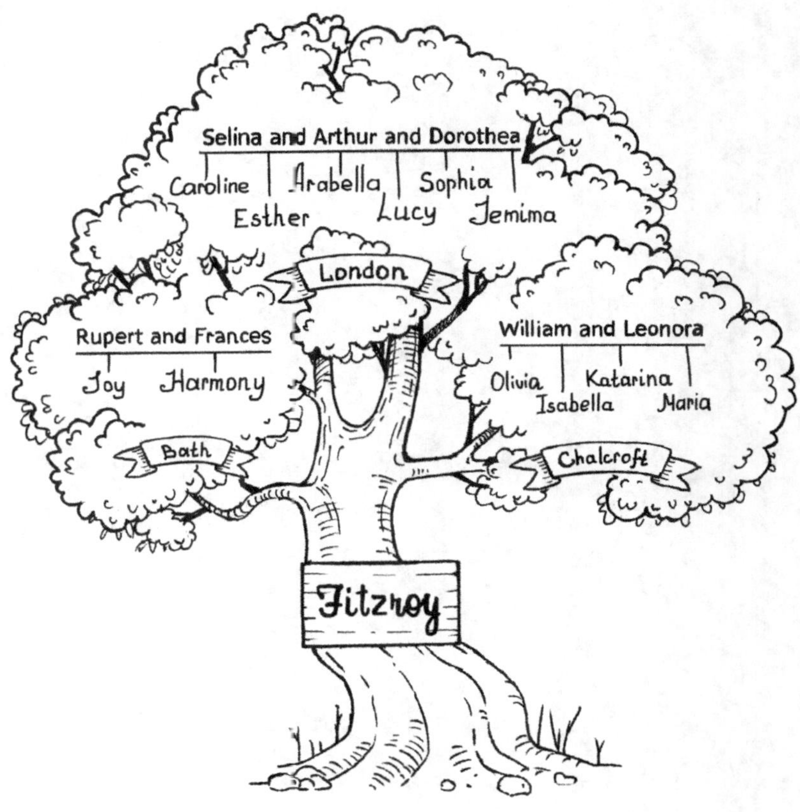

Selina and Arthur and Dorothea
Caroline
Arabella
Sophia
Esther
Lucy
Jemima
London
Rupert and Frances
Joy
Harmony
William and Leonora
Olivia
Katarina
Isabella
Maria
Bath
Chalcroft
Fitzroy

CHAPTER ONE

THERE WAS SOMETHING incredibly familiar about the handwriting Harmony Fitzroy could see on the outside of the letter.

One of the corners was slightly damp from the snow falling heavily past the morning room window. Her sister Joy was seated there at the desk, her back to the room. She had not even looked up when the morning's post had been delivered, and neither had their mother, sitting on the sofa at the other end of the room.

Book cast aside, Harmony stared at the letter, puzzled. She had not been expecting a letter from any of her acquaintances. Surely if it were important, it would have been addressed to her mother?

"If you are not going to open it," Joy spoke unexpectedly with a tired tone in her voice, "then may I suggest that you put it on the fire? This room is freezing."

Harmony smiled; she knew better than to take Joy too seriously. Her wandering fingers circled the letter and felt the soft roll of wax that was the seal. Who could it be from?

Snow continued to fall onto the streets of Bath. Rather than look at the mysterious letter, Harmony allowed her gaze to drift around the room. Her sister's golden hair had been expertly pinned up, so it fell just like the snowdrifts on Milsom Street that morning.

Harmony herself had chosen her favorite pastel pink gown though she regretted it now she saw herself in the morning room, decorated as it was with pastel pink and creams. The wallpaper was a delicate rose color, and although the flooring was cream, the furniture was all picked out in delicate pink silks.

If Harmony stayed very still, it was as if she was not there at all—something that she often attempted when her shyness overcame her.

"Now, Joy," said their mother gently as she turned the page of the novel she was reading, "I am sure if you are that cold, I can ask Mrs. Bird to bring some coal in for the fire."

"Mind me not," said Joy, not turning round but waving a hand in the air. "Just promise to defrost me in the spring."

Harmony caught her mother's eye, and they smiled at each other. Frances Fitzroy knew better than to take her eldest daughter's words to heart. She raised a quizzical brow at Harmony and looked at the letter. Harmony could not help but blush—though she knew not why.

Well, thought Harmony silently, there is no earthly way to tell who this letter is from, save by opening it.

It took but five seconds, and as soon as she glanced at the name at the bottom of the letter, she sighed with relief. It was from her music teacher, Monsieur Bernard; he had not written to her before, and part of her assumed he had misdirected his letter—surely it had been intended for her father, Rupert?

But as Harmony began to read, she realized that was certainly not the case. Hands clutching the letter, she crumpled one side in her excitement. Her breathing quickened. She had misread it, surely. It could not be.

"Well?"

Even Joy's sarcastic temper could not dampen Harmony's exhilaration.

"'Tis from Monsieur Bernard," she said, trying to keep the excitement from her voice. Was she reading it correctly? Surely he could not be asking her—but there it was, in plain English, and in a beautiful hand:

> *My dear Mademoiselle Fitzroy,*
>
> *Each year I know you attend the Assembly Rooms' Christmas Eve concert with the rest of my pupils, but this year I now consider your musical skill to be proficient enough to join my musical ensemble.*
>
> *We shall be performing Bach, of course—I know he is a favorite of yours, so I look to you to practice, and we will discuss the exact running order at our next lesson, appointed for this Thursday at 3 o'clock in the afternoon.*
>
> *I am, your ever devoted servant,*
> *Pierre Bernard*

Harmony's eyes were a light sky blue, a trait that she had inherited from her father, and anyone looking at her at this very moment could not help but call them sapphires, rather than mere irises. Tears swam beneath them as Harmony read the short letter again.

The Christmas Eve concert was attended so well that it was almost a religion in Bath, where she and her family dwelled.

Despite being part of a family that could only just hold a Christmas carol near enough to its tune to be recognizable, Harmony had somehow come by a rather large amount of musical talent—not something she would ever own aloud, but something that she knew, deep inside her.

Her family had joked, of course, about her weekly music lessons with Monsieur Bernard, but now: now they would be able to see her perform, and in public, too! This was not something that most women were accorded—and to be given the honor, at just seventeen!

Harmony swallowed. In public. Before other people.

It was an honor, she had to keep remembering that. That, or her breakfast would make a reappearance.

"Ah, Monsieur Bernard," said their mother warmly, laying

down her book. "I trust he is quite well? He has not sought to cancel your music lesson this week due to illness?"

Harmony swallowed, and she cast her eyes down to the letter one more time, just to be sure.

"He…" She swallowed again, her hesitation drawing even Joy's curiosity. Her ruby gown, made from the finest of muslin, rustled as she turned to face Harmony.

Harmony cleared her throat. It was only her mother and sister; she should have the courage to speak before them! "Monsieur Bernard has invited me to be part of the Christmas Eve concert at the Assembly Rooms this year!"

Her words did not have the desired effect.

"Oh, good," said Joy, her eyes immediately glazing over, and she turned back to the letter she was writing. "Do you have any news for Olivia?"

Harmony knew better than to be offended—after all, none of her family save her mother, had ever accompanied her to the Christmas Eve concert, despite it being such an occasion for the Season, but she had hoped for a more exciting response.

"Joy," Harmony repeated, "I have received an invitation for the concert."

Joy did not look round. "Invitation? You go every year, why should you worry about an invitation?"

Harmony sighed heavily. Smoothing her gown with shaking fingers, she rose and walked over to the desk in the window where Joy was writing.

"Not that kind of invitation," said Harmony as she sat in the window seat and looked up at her sister. "This is an invitation to…to take part."

Joy did not look up; she was slightly biting her lip as she wrote.

Harmony sighed once more. "Joy, are you even listening? They have asked me to play, as one of the musicians!"

Joy's head snapped up. "Play?"

Harmony nodded. If she was not careful, the tears of happiness she had been desperately trying to quell would fall.

To play music, and in public! Such a distinction…she could not recall a woman ever playing in public like that, unless she was a great virtuoso—and then usually only singers.

Tension grew in her shoulders, but she tried to ignore it. She was pleased. It was more than she had ever dreamed.

"Harmony, that is wonderful!" Joy's smile was genuine, and she reached out a hand to clasp her sister's.

She looked at her mother, but she saw that she had already fixed a smile on her face.

"Darling, that is good news," she said, her hands already moving to pick up the book laid down by her side. "Do let me know if you need the carriage that evening."

"But," said Harmony, more hopefully than expectantly, "you will surely want to come, and listen?"

"Of course, I would, dear." Frances Fitzroy's voice emanated from behind the cover of a book Harmony did not recognize.

Harmony tried to smile, but it was not easy. Could she not see how exciting this was? Surely her mother would think differently when she had finished the riveting tale in her hands.

"But Mother," she tried again, "to be invited to play at the Christmas Eve concert—'tis an honor many musicians long for, and there are many much older and more experienced than I who have surely been passed aside!"

"That's a shame, dear," her mother spoke absentmindedly, clearly not paying heed to her words.

Harmony turned toward her sister. Surely Joy, who had suffered through most of her practicing years as a child, would understand.

But Joy preempted her plea. "Do not even think on it, Harmony," she said quietly, still writing. "You know it would bore me to tears, and you being the one playing would, I'm afraid, certainly not endear the concert to me."

"Please, it would mean so much to me!" Harmony's face was desperate, her tone pleading, but there did not seem to be anything she could do to persuade her sister. "Joy, I am asking you as a sister," said Harmony with a sigh. "Please attend the concert."

Joy looked up irritably, pen in hand. "Harmony, you ask us this every year. Every Christmas you ask me to attend the Christmas Eve concert, despite knowing full well that music is not something that I can appreciate like you do, yet you hound me with the same question."

Harmony looked at her sister with a faint smile on her face. Ever the exaggerator was her sister. "I do not hound you, Joy, that is a little strong."

"Or not strong enough," said Joy archly, turning her back on her sister and lowering pen to paper once more.

Harmony stared at the back of her sister's head. Her own hair was not as tidy as Joy's, although just as brilliantly gold.

At the age of seventeen, Harmony had always thought that, by now, this sort of argument would have had a foregone conclusion—in her favor. But Joy, three years her elder, had a strong will that was not to be brooked.

But this year was different.

Harmony looked down once more at the letter from Monsieur Bernard.

Each year I know you attend the Assembly Rooms' Christmas Eve concert with the rest of my pupils, but this year I now consider your musical skill to be proficient enough to join my musical ensemble.

Joy sighed once more. "Do not be downcast, Harmony. I had no idea that you were being considered for such an honor!"

"What honor?"

The door to the morning room opened, and two young women entered.

"Esther, Lucy!" Harmony could not wait to tell them the news. "I have been invited to play as a musician in the Christmas Eve concert!"

Too late, Harmony realized that her cousins Esther and Lucy would probably have no understanding at all about the real meaning of her words. After all, they did not live in Bath and were London bred.

Harmony and Joy, however, had never lived elsewhere and had lived and breathed Bath for so long it was strange to think there was anywhere else—and to think that someone in the world may not appreciate the Christmas Eve concert!

"That's wonderful!" Esther, her flame-red hair almost coming undone from her hasty pins in the rush she made toward her cousin, smiled brightly.

She threw herself rather indelicately next to her aunt, who merely rustled a page. Harmony could see that her white gown, almost a uniform for Esther—had become sopping wet at the hem due to the snow outside.

"I would imagine that this is a great honor, rarely afforded to anyone," said Esther with a little hesitation. "Is that right?"

"Rarely afforded to any man!" Harmony said with a smile. "I do not think I have ever heard or seen a woman as part of the ensemble."

"And they have asked you?" Lucy was only a year younger than she was, but Harmony almost felt as though she was her twin, they were so similar in character. "Harmony, my darling, I am so proud of you!"

Joy was impressed enough by the rapturous praise of her cousins, Harmony saw, to actually lay down her pen—which was saying something, as she was writing to another one of their cousins.

It was a rather sprawling family, the Fitzroys. Three brothers had produced twelve daughters, cousins who frequently visited each other at Christmas and in the summer.

While Esther and Lucy's father—and their four other sisters—lived in London, Harmony and Joy had made Bath their home forever. Their Uncle William, head of the family, held the seat at Chalcroft along with his four daughters—one of whom,

Olivia, was Joy's correspondent.

"I simply must tell Caroline, once I've finished this note to Olivia," said Joy, her fingers clearly itching to get back to her letter.

"And tell her that we are still waiting for our gloves to be posted on!" Esther cut over the babble between Lucy and Harmony, discussing which music was to be played. "As our eldest sister, it is really her responsibility to make sure they arrive, and they certainly have not!"

Harmony sat down on the chaise longue, almost exhausted with excitement.

She was to play in the Christmas Eve concert. Her!

"I suppose it will be some very long pieces of music?" Joy questioned without turning round.

Harmony gave Lucy a knowing look, and she had to stifle her giggles.

"Almost certainly, yes, hours and hours," said Harmony, smiling at Esther as she came to sit beside her. "I would imagine that they will choose Pleyel, and perhaps Mozart, and even Handel if there is room in the repertoire—Monsieur mentions only Bach, but there is undoubtedly to be more."

She would have to begin practicing immediately—perhaps this very moment. A flicker of fear seared her heart. What if she made a mistake? What if she ruined a piece with a discord, ruined the entire concert?

Perhaps it would be best if she did not perform. Perhaps she should write back to Monsieur Bernard and—

"Goodness," said Lucy, looking slightly alarmed. "Are you not anxious you may play something wrong?"

Too late, Lucy saw the warning signs from her sister Esther.

Lucy blushed. "Not that I think you will have a problem—after all, you are the best musician in the family."

"And that is saying something," said Joy drily, "as there are plenty of us."

But Harmony could not be cut by Joy's remarks today, not

when she had received such wonderful news. "I am so happy, and I cannot wait to be playing there, in the Assembly Rooms, and look up to see you all seated there, smiling at me!"

It was as though someone had dropped a rather delicate and beautiful champagne flute; the silence was awkward, deep, and no one quite knew where to look.

"You are…you are coming, aren't you Esther?" Harmony took the hand of her cousin seated beside her, but Esther was already trying to avoid her gaze.

"The thing is," said Esther quietly, "I am more likely to fall asleep than be able to enjoy the music you play, Harmony. You know none of us are musical."

"And I would not want to fall asleep in the middle of your concert," said Lucy with an earnest tone in her voice. "It would be the height of rudeness. I would be so ashamed!"

"You could just try to stay awake," said Harmony, trying not to let the bitterness creep into her voice.

Perhaps the best day of her life, and none of her family thought to join her in her triumph?

Joy laughed. "Easier said than done, little sister. You are the only Fitzroy with any ear for music, you cannot quite appreciate how difficult we find it to follow."

"But I want you all to be there." Harmony looked around the room and saw only awkward and slightly shameful faces looking back at her—including her own mother's. "It is going to be such a special moment, not one I can repeat, and I want to share it with you."

Harmony looked beseechingly at her sister, mother, and two cousins in turn.

"Blast it," said Joy with a sign of resignation. "I will be there— but only if we agree to only speak of this for five minutes a day, or you shall wear me out completely!"

Harmony squealed with joy and cast a beaming smile toward her sister. It went completely unnoticed, as Joy had already returned to her letter, but Harmony felt as though wings had erupted from her back and had lifted her up to the heights of the clouds.

Joy would be there!

"And we'll come, of course." Esther and Lucy had agreed between them while Harmony had been distracted.

"Even if we do fall asleep," giggled Lucy.

Harmony could not help but laugh. "If you start to snore, Lucy Fitzroy, I shall leave off playing and come over to shake you!"

The three girls laughed, and Joy's words were barely heard over their amusement.

"At least if we meet some nice gentlemen," she said with a wicked smile, bent over her letter, "the evening shall not be completely wasted!"

Chapter Two

THE HEADACHE BUILDING at the very front of Harmony's forehead was starting to distract her.

Each of her fingers ached, but she could not draw herself away from the pianoforte. Not yet. Not until she had mastered this particularly difficult phrasing that really made the melody sing…

She had been seated at the pianoforte in their drawing room for above three hours but was just as unsatisfied with her performance as when she had first sat down.

Harmony blinked, trying to ignore the stabbing pains around her eyes, tired from constantly rubbing them between movements. The window to the street outside was directly to her right, and normally she welcomed any natural light and the ability to see what was going on in the world around her. But not today. Today it was not enough.

"Just one more time through," she muttered to herself, unconsciously taking on a little of the French accent typical of her musical tutor, Monsieur Bernard. "Once through, with no mistakes, and you may go."

Her fingers gently stroked the keys she knew so well, as she tried to focus on the sheet music before her. Expensive to come by, especially for a player as voracious as Harmony, she and Joy had taken it in turns—one sister willingly, the other with reticence—to copy out the pieces which really caught her eye.

She took in a breath, raised her elbows slightly simultaneously, and began the piece by Bach. He was one of her favorite composers, and it was a piece that she knew well, the English Suite, written for harpsichord and now performed on the pianoforte. It was one that on a normal day she would revel in.

This was not a normal day.

Her fingers seemed heavy, nimbleness gone, the ability of her fingers to keep up with the movement of her eyes across the page totally lost.

A discord, a harsh sound as a note that was not meant to be there, crept into the melody. Harmony winced, then winced again as she heard another. Finally, she'd had enough.

"Blast it all!" Her words were violent, and she was frustrated enough to push the parchment from the pianoforte in anger. They fluttered softly to the floor.

The more nervous I get, thought Harmony anxiously, *the worse I am becoming; and I have only known about the invitation to take part in the Christmas Eve concert but a day. There are almost three weeks until the performance itself. How on earth will I be able to play then?*

"I am not rattled," she said quietly to the empty room. It had become a habit of hers when she was younger, when she could not persuade Joy to sit in and listen to her practice. "I am not frightened, I am just practicing."

Another piece of music caught her eye, a steadier, arguably easier piece by Ignaz Pleyel. Surely her struggling fingers would be able to make light work of it.

The confidence she always felt when seated on this soft leather seemed to be lacking, but Harmony blamed it on the lack of light. The afternoon sun had been quickly conquered by the gathering clouds, and she had only been permitted two candles to help guide her through the music.

Harmony coughed and stretched her fingers out before she placed them back on the keyboard. "Take a deep breath," she instructed herself quietly, "and sing the music through your fingers."

The first note was struck, the first chord created, and although each movement was technically correct, Harmony had too much of a musician's ear to ignore the fact that there seemed to be no soul in her playing.

It was all accurately corresponding to the notes on the paper before her, but the magic, the delight in her playing, was gone.

The last note sounded, and it was finished.

Harmony placed her hands in her lap and stared dully at the music. Ignaz Pleyel was a composer for children. If she could not inspire greatness from that, there was really no point in her even attempting the Christmas Eve concert. Unless…

Decision made, Harmony stood up and accidentally ripped the Bach music—but she did not notice. She stepped into the hall and took down her dark red pelisse which perfectly matched the coral gown she had put on that morning.

"Mother!" She called whilst she struggled to pull one of the sleeves the right way out.

Her mother's voice returned from somewhere in the house. "Yes, child?"

"I am going to visit Monsieur Bernard," said Harmony. She did not expect to see her mother; she had informed the family at breakfast, much to Esther and Lucy's amusement, that she had reached a most exciting chapter in her novel, and she was not to be disturbed all day. "I shall not be long."

"Whatever you want, my dear," was the only reply that Harmony received.

She stood in the hall and took one look at herself in the looking glass that they kept by the door.

Harmony smiled, and her reflection smiled back at her. She would fix this. She would.

She had to.

It would take her but moments to reach Monsieur Bernard's house, as it was only two streets away. Since she had turned fifteen, Harmony had been permitted by her parents to go to

Monsieur Bernard's alone and unaccompanied. Partly, Harmony suspected with a smile in the cold damp late afternoon in December, because Joy had put up such a fuss about having to wait around for her younger sister to finish her lessons.

Harmony wove through the winter crowds. It really did seem as though the entire world had come to Bath for the Season, and Harmony did not believe there was room enough for them all!

Everywhere she looked she saw new faces, faces which had quite clearly just stepped off a carriage into the most fashionable city of England—but Harmony had no time to stand around to be part of the picturesque scene.

She did not have an appointment to see Monsieur Bernard, of course, but Harmony did not mind waiting. After knocking at his door, his butler recognized her immediately.

"Miss Fitzroy," he said in a gravelly tone, bowing and opening the door so that she could slip inside. "Monsieur is expecting you?"

"No, Malham," she said with a hint of a smile. The shyness that had crippled her in her youth only surfaced occasionally, but it was something she tried to keep hidden. Malham, of course, she had known for years. That did not matter. "But I am happy to wait in the morning room if that is agreeable?"

Malham did not reply, only bowed.

Harmony knew him and the house well enough. She strode forward and opened the second door on the right of the hallway and relaxed as the warmth of the fire in the grate immediately met her.

She never grew bored when waiting for Monsieur Bernard; there was so much to see in his home. A refugee from France, Monsieur Bernard had been so fortunate as to bring almost his entire estate with him when he fled from the Terror, and he had never parted with a single item that he could not find space for.

Every inch of every room was cluttered with maps, clocks, small brass metal items that Harmony did not know the use of, papers written in French, and some in German, scraps of music that did not seem to have any date or title.

Everywhere that she looked, a surface was taken up with a memento of a town, a person, a time in his life. You could create a museum of Monsieur Bernard, Harmony thought with a smile, and you could fill it amply with the contents of just one room.

Moving aside two books on the German Baroque period from the sofa in the center of the room, Harmony perched herself on the end and looked at the stuffed pheasant that was delicately and rather precariously balanced over the fireplace.

Beside it sat a large plate that was covered in sandwiches that looked suspiciously moldy, and on the other side was a silver plate dedicated to St. Cecelia.

Harmony had always loved this room because as well as having a door to the hallway, there was another door to the music room.

When she had first come to Monsieur Bernard as a child, much to the chagrin of her parents, who did not believe they could have possibly produced a musically proficient child, she had sat right where she was sitting now, listening to the older students playing, eyes closed, drinking it all in.

In fact, she could hear someone in the music room now, playing what sounded like the pipe—although not like any pipe she had heard before.

The lilting melody was absolutely beautiful. Surely an instrument could not create such heavenly music? She had never heard such soaring notes, almost like a soprano singing.

Harmony could not help it. Curiosity and shyness combined in one person was most unfortunate, but there it was.

She could see from the sofa that the door to the music room was slightly ajar. Creeping over the scattered cushions and the clarinet lying on the floor, she moved silently toward the door for a glimpse inside—and gasped.

There was a musician in there whom she had never seen before. He was tall, with dark hair and a slight brush of dark fuzz across his cheeks and chin. He wore a coat of the latest fashion, made from rich and expensive cloth, and he was playing the piccolo in the middle of the room with his eyes closed as though his life depended on it.

Harmony tried to keep her gasp quiet, hoping the beautiful music the gentleman was making would prevent him from hearing her.

She could not help but stare. How was it possible that just one person could play such a searingly beautiful melody? Her knowledge of the piccolo was little, and yet it did not seem humanly possible to be able to create the depth of tone and variety of notes he was.

Harmony drank in the music as though it was feeding her very soul, watching the musician curiously.

He did not look much older than she, but there was a certain way he stood that demonstrated his confidence, which surely could only have come from age. She could not see the color of his eyes, for though he had entered into a new movement, he had not needed to take one single look at the page, his eyes remaining closed.

He was handsome, his strong hands expertly moving around the piccolo delicately and yet with a strength of purpose that was incredible.

Harmony bit her lip. Watching him secretly like this made her entire body feel warm and strange. A heat was blossoming in her stomach and between her legs. He was majestic.

If she should be caught here—if someone should walk in from the hallway and see her watching this gentleman in what was, as she knew, one of the most intimate positions a musician could be in, there would be a very awkward conversation.

As much as she hated to, Harmony tore her eyes away from him and took a step back—right onto a cymbal she had not noticed.

Wincing, Harmony tried to take another step backward so she could at least pretend she had been seated, but as the tempo of her heart increased in her ears, the door before her opened fully, and the musician she had been watching standing in the doorway.

Harmony just stared at him.

Now his gaze was fixed upon her, piccolo in his hands, she could see his eyes were a sparkling gray. Harmony could not stop staring at him. He was perfect, the most handsome man she had ever seen—though the beautiful music he had been playing, which was still ringing in her ears, might have played a part in that.

Harmony blinked. She did not appear to be able to stop looking at him.

The gentleman coughed, awkwardly.

"Good afternoon," he said in a smooth, quiet voice. "I did not realize I had an audience."

Harmony managed to will her mouth to open, but she did not seem able to force words from her mind to her tongue. Her jaw hung there, open, like a fool.

Say something, she cried silently to herself. *Please, anything!*

The man shuffled his feet. "I am David Navarre," he said softly, a slight smile emerging onto his face. "And you are?"

Harmony swallowed and tried again. "H-Harmony. Harmony Fitzroy."

She cursed the nerves she always hoped to conquer. It was most unfair that she could say nothing eloquent with such a gentleman before her.

If Joy were here, she would say something witty, and Mr. Navarre would smile, perhaps laugh. They would fall into an amusing conversation, and he would leave her presence wondering if he could see her again.

And here she was, standing mute, unable to say anything. Barely able to say her own name!

Harmony attempted to speak again in a more natural tone. For some reason, she was incredibly aware of her body—her toes squeezed together in her shoes, her shoulders tight with embarrassment, her hands just hanging there, on either side of her.

She had to concentrate to stop herself from swaying. "I must apologize for listening to you play, I…I-I was just so taken by the music."

"Handel," said Mr. Navarre, "one of my particular favorites, I have to say."

"Yes, I know," said Harmony eagerly—and at the sight of his furrowed brow, explained, "I mean, I was aware it was Handel. His Water Music, am I correct?"

Mr. Navarre nodded, not taking his eyes from her.

Harmony took a shallow breath. He was staring at her because she had intruded. That was all.

"And yet…yet it is not an arrangement I recognize," Harmony managed. "One of your own invention?"

Now a truly genuine smile spread across his features. "It is indeed, although not one I have performed in public. You are my first recital."

Embarrassment and shame flushed right through Harmony. "I must sincerely apologize, Mr. Navarre, I had no idea! I would be mortified if someone had heard me before I was ready to present a piece to the world, you must accept my apologies—"

"You are a musician also?" Mr. Navarre cut across her. He took a small step toward her, and Harmony unconsciously matched the distance by taking a step back. "What instrument do you favor?"

There seemed to be very little space between them, and Harmony tried to concentrate on her breathing, keeping the feelings which felt like panic, but surely couldn't be, at bay.

It was wild to panic at speaking with a gentleman—but then, this was a very unusual circumstance.

She could not recall a similar one. Speaking with a gentleman before one was formally introduced? More, speaking with him alone?

Mr. Navarre took another step toward her. Harmony swallowed.

"I…I play the…" *The words were simple enough,* she scolded herself silently, *so why can I not articulate them?*

But she was saved, as chance would have it, by the opening of the door behind her.

"Ah, Monsieur Navarre!" Monsieur Bernard strode across the room, stepping indiscriminately on whatever his feet touched. Both Harmony and Mr. Navarre winced at the cracking of the newspaper that had been lying on the floor innocently enough. "I'd hoped you would have begun, yet I hear no beautiful water *musique. Pourquoi?"*

Harmony had turned on the spot when Monsieur Bernard had entered and was about to explain—for the second time, and in just as awkward circumstances—that she had interrupted Mr. Navarre's practice, but he was too quick for her.

"Miss Fitzroy and I were discussing the various merits of displaying new music to an audience," he said easily. "And it is a delight, as ever, to meet another of your pupils, Monsieur Bernard."

"Ah, my clever friend!" Monsieur Bernard was not a tall man, but he made up for it in sheer presence, giving a cheeky wink to Harmony who could not help but smile. "But who is the real teacher, *mon amie,* when you play as well as you do?"

"I am ever hopeful of learning," replied Mr. Navarre.

Harmony could see his smile was genuine, and it transformed his face. None of his striking good looks were altered, but they seemed to spark alive.

"In fact, I was about to invite Miss Fitzroy to accompany me at tomorrow afternoon's recital in the Pump Room."

Monsieur Bernard beamed as Harmony's face fell. "Ah, Monsieur Navarre that is a capital idea, *très bien!* Do not worry Miss Harmony, I shall explain the *musique* in two short moments, it is nothing you have not tried before!"

He pushed past them and entered the music room, shouting over his shoulder, "I have the *musique* for you somewhere!"

Harmony heard a loud crash as Monsieur Bernard started

hunting for the sheet music, but she could not take her eyes from David Navarre's face.

"How did you know?" She spoke in barely a whisper, unable to manage more, unwilling to be overheard by her music teacher. "How could you possibly know I play the pianoforte?"

Mr. Navarre smiled, reached forward, and raised her left hand before him. "Never underestimate the beauty in a pianist's fingers."

Before Harmony had a moment to register the searing heat from the contact between them, the moment was over; he let go, and then strode past her out in the hallway.

"Tomorrow. Two o'clock. Sharp."

Chapter Three

Rupert Fitzroy strode into the breakfast room the next morning with a smile on his face and a letter in his hand.

"Morning Fitzroys!" he said breezily to the gaggle of women currently adorning his home.

Various were his replies. Harmony looked up at her father and smiled as cheerful and merry "Good mornings" were uttered from her cousins. There was a glare from Joy, who had clearly been slighted by someone in the last few minutes, and nothing at all from her mother, his wife, who was currently two-thirds of the way through a very sticky and buttery book.

"Is that a letter for all of us, Father?" Joy asked, staring at the fluttering pages. "If private, I would take care not to flap it about before us, else we shall end up reading the majority of it from here."

"Smile, Joy, it's good for your heart," said her father good-naturedly as he sat down.

Esther and Lucy giggled. Their uncle was certainly more lighthearted and more quizzical than their father, and during their stays—sadly infrequent, as their mother simply couldn't spare them—they delighted in the myriad of nonsense he was almost certain to utter.

"Much good it would do me," retorted Joy, letting her cutlery fall to the table with a clatter. "You know, the season has been underway for nigh on three months, and we have had a complete dearth of invitations."

"Now, Joy," said Esther with a smile as she passed over some hot chocolate to her sister across the table. Her typical white dress was today adorned with a light blue ribbon, tied just under the bust, and a pair of sapphire ear bobs that matched. "There is more than enough time for balls—and I thought you more determined to scorn those who counted time by merriment and outings?"

"And so I am," Joy replied nonchalantly, retrieving her cutlery.

Harmony could not help but smile. Joy's very problem so often was that she was, at heart, better-natured than anyone she had ever met. She just loved to air her views, and once they were out, it was as though they fluttered away like mist.

"Yet there must be something to do around here. We are not men," said Joy irritably. "We cannot simply stroll about town and decide to join a club, or play sport, or go out riding. There are countless and endless female occupations, but do they have to be so dull?"

"I have my music," said Harmony quietly, "more than enough to keep me entertained."

"Reading," was the short contribution her mother made to the conversation, and no one paid much attention.

One of the things that Harmony loved about her family was their conversation. Admittedly, when her mother was engaged in the topic of conversation, it was more lively. But even this morning in the breakfast room, painted in the soft creams that Bath was so well known for, the room always seemed bright, spacious, and ready for words to flow.

The topics themselves, of course, could never be predicted.

"That is why I have decided," announced Joy in a rather somber tone, "to marry."

There was stunned silence after this pronouncement, during which Esther and Lucy exchanged gleeful glances, and Harmony looked at her sister in surprise.

"Goodness," she said, "I had not realized you were previously avoiding it!"

"Anyone in particular in mind?" Rupert always enjoyed poking fun at his daughters, and as Joy was offering herself as this morning's sport, so much the better. "I assume half the fun is deciding on exactly to whom."

"No one in particular," said Joy.

Harmony realized, with a sinking feeling, that her face was completely humorless. *This is not a game*, she thought. *Joy is serious.*

Joy was still speaking. "If I were married, I might have more freedom. No offense, Father," she added hastily.

"Oh, nonsense," said her father briskly, "and on the note of marriage, I have a rather amusing letter from my brother, Arthur."

Esther pricked up as she heard her father's name. "From Papa?"

Rupert Fitzroy nodded. "The very same! To think, he has finally been approached for the hand of one of his daughters, and it has taken a full week for the news to arrive."

"Hand?" Lucy sat bolt upright, almost spilling raspberry jam all down her Spanish blue cotton gown. "Who is it?"

"It must be Caroline," said Harmony eagerly, "surely it must be her, she is the only one of you I can think of who even has a suitor!"

"Old Walsingham," said Esther with a frown. "I suppose so, though a boring old doctor is not the sort of man I would have wished for her."

"As long as it's not Jemima," snorted Lucy, "I think I should suffer an apoplexy if it be her!"

Harmony giggled with her cousins. Caroline was the eldest of the six sisters in that branch of the family, with Jemima, her half-sister, coming just a month before. Caroline's mother had another daughter, Esther, and was then widowed; and a year later, she married Jemima's father. Arabella, Lucy, and Sophia then swiftly followed.

"Remind me," said Joy curiously, "what was his name?"

"Caroline's young follower? Stuart Walsingham—Dr. Stuart Walsingham, I suppose I should say," said Esther. "Is it her, Uncle Rupert?"

He held all of their attention for a moment, to the point that even his wife Frances looked up from her book, then he nodded.

Lucy clapped her hands as both Harmony and Joy exclaimed their happiness. Esther was the quietest. Closest to Caroline in age, Esther looked a little piqued. Perhaps, Harmony guessed, she was saddened to hear the news of her sister's engagement secondhand. The celebrations would be over by the time the sisters returned to London.

"When will the wedding occur?" Frances asked over her novel. "The spring?"

Rupert waved his hand vaguely, the letter fluttering through the air. "Arthur gives no details, he just says young Walsingham—that is exactly how he refers to him, the old man—young Walsingham has asked permission both of himself and of his daughter, and both, thankfully, have accepted."

"I have news also," said Harmony suddenly, remembering she had not yet mentioned her latest news to any of her family.

Unfortunately, her meager words were not sufficient to keep her mother interested, who disappeared under the intrigue of her latest chapter.

But Joy smiled. "More news?"

Harmony waited a moment to gather her thoughts. She had to ensure, as best she could, that her cheeks would not flush. "I have been asked to accompany a small chamber orchestra this afternoon at the Pump Room. Accompany a piccolo player."

"My word, you dark horse!" Joy laughed at the sight of her sister blushing. "Who is she, this piccolo player?"

"Ugh, a recital!" Lucy asked, screwing up her forehead. "It sounds a most horrible chore!"

"That it is," answered Harmony's father with a chuckle, "yet most of the time, Harmony does not mind. 'Tis the first time you have been requested as an accompaniment, however. What's her name?"

Harmony swallowed, the rhythm of the conversation slowing, then said the words she knew would bring the merriment of the table to a complete halt. "David. David Navarre."

She was completely right in her estimation.

"David Navarre?" Suddenly the lively tone in her father's voice evaporated. "That does not sound like the sort of young woman I want you accompanying."

"David?" Joy's eyes widened. "Lord, Harmony, I did not know you had a young gentleman friend!"

"I don't!" Harmony blurted, panic filling her mind.

All she had been able to think about was playing with David—with Mr. Navarre this afternoon, visions of the subtle way he coaxed such stunning music out of the strings had been all she could concentrate on.

She and Mr. Navarre, performing together. In public.

It was but the Pump Rooms, to be sure, but there would be people there. Society. She would be seen playing with a gentleman.

"It is just a performance," Harmony said quietly. "He is young—perhaps Joy's age, or a bit older—and Monsieur Bernard is aware of the plans, and he will be there. Papa, there will be nothing…nothing untoward."

Silence fell as all at the table turned to look at Rupert.

Lucy whispered to Joy, "I would never have thought it of Harmony!"

Harmony's cheeks darkened. She had never done anything so bold in her life, that was true, but she had no wish to bring scandal to her name, nor that of her family's.

But the thought of playing with David, their music entwining…

"Please, Father," said Harmony quietly, her eyes fixed on

those of her father's. "It is a real accolade to play in the Pump Room, and I would be loath to miss it."

Rupert pondered for a moment. "Who is this David Navarre? What do you know of him?"

"Absolutely nothing, I am afraid," she said apologetically. If only she had asked questions at the time, but she had been barely able to string two words together. "But Monsieur Bernard thinks well of him and seemed most eager for us to play together."

"Most musicians are down on their luck and desperate for money," said Rupert calmly.

Harmony took great offense at this. "Do I look down on my luck and desperate for money?"

This statement drew gentle giggles from the younger members of the table and caused a crack of a smile to break on Rupert's face.

"Well, no my dear, not as such," he admitted, "but I want you to promise me you will hold yourself with the utmost decorum."

"Yes, Father."

"And that your sister will go with you."

"Yes, Father."

"Hold on a moment!" protested Joy. "I didn't agree to that!"

Rupert laughed. "Sorry, Joy, but I am going to have to ask you to play chaperone!"

From where Harmony was sitting, it did not look as though it was a delight to Joy, but her concern for her sister quickly dissipated. She was going to be playing in just five short hours with David Navarre.

HARMONY LOOKED AROUND and tried to commit everything that was about her to memory.

She could smell the resin from Mr. Navarre's case, see the

flautist gently slotting his instrument together, hear the gentle note of the clarinet, holding a C so others could tune.

Every time she looked across the room, her eyes swam with all the people promenading up and down, casting curious looks at her, the only female musician of the six.

She shifted slightly on the high leather seat, and she gently stroked the keys of the pianoforte.

Every instrument was different, one of the curses of those who played such an instrument was that they had to adapt to each one they came across.

Harmony shot a look at David Navarre, seated beside her. He glanced over at her. She flushed and looked away.

Though Monsieur Bernard had been quite explicit in his instructions as to time and place, he had failed to mention any particular clothing she should wear, and she wished he had.

Now she saw Mr. Navarre and the other musicians, she realized she should have inquired. All were dressed smartly in red waistcoats embroidered delicately with golden thread, all with red cravats—though each man had chosen his own particular knot. Her own simple red gown was without gold adornments, but at least was the same shade of claret.

Harmony stole another look at Mr. Navarre beside her.

Lovingly and carefully, Mr. Navarre had pulled his piccolo out of its case and was now running his fingers up and down the keys as though they were a well-worn path to a view that he loved.

There was nothing but confidence on his face, as though he belonged there, seated in front of some of the best society of England. The dark stubble on his cheeks had disappeared, but there was already a shadow appearing along his jawline.

Harmony swallowed. Her throat was dry.

She fixed her eyes on the sheet music Monsieur Bernard had placed there only moments ago, but it swam in front of her eyes. She could taste bile in the back of her throat, and for one awful moment, she really thought that she was going to vomit.

"Are you quite well, Miss Fitzroy?"

The voice that had spoken was gentle, and it took Harmony a few moments to realize the words had come from Mr. Navarre. He was gazing at her with a concerned look, nothing but kindness in his eyes.

Harmony swallowed, trying to moisten her lips. "Quite well, I thank you, Mr. Navarre. It is just…" She took another look around the room and willed herself to keep talking. "I have not played in public before."

Mr. Navarre lowered his piccolo slightly and moved closer to her.

Harmony breathed in his scent: musk and sandalwood and a spice she did not know.

"Truly—this is your first performance?"

He sounded so concerned, Harmony could not help but smile with embarrassment. "As shameful as it is to own, Mr. Navarre, I am not at home in public, whether it be speaking or playing! This is something I have no experience of, and I fear—" Her words caught in her throat, but she pushed through. "I fear I shall let you and the other musicians down."

She cast her eyes around the group.

Besides herself, Mr. Navarre on the piccolo, and the young man now experimentally running through his scales on the flute, there was an elderly gentleman with a cello, another man, perhaps a little older than Mr. Navarre, with a violin, and a man closer to her own age on the clarinet. All looked supremely confident.

Harmony returned her gaze to Mr. Navarre, who had an odd expression on his face. Was it pity?

"Fear not, Miss Fitzroy," he said quietly, leaning toward her under the pretense of shuffling through some music. "I would not have asked you to join us if I truly believed you were unable to rise to the challenge. Consider this the prelude to your splendid performance on Christmas Eve."

"But you know nothing about me!" Harmony blurted. "You

have not even heard me play in private, let alone perform in public with a group of musicians I have never rehearsed with! How can you have such faith in me?"

"I don't know," said Mr. Navarre after a pause, casting her a brilliant smile. "Is that not strange?"

Harmony opened her mouth to reply, but she was instantly distracted by the elder violinist subtly tapping his bow on the music stand.

This was their call to action; no conductor was required in this setting, and Harmony knew the performance was about to begin.

Almost in a panic, Harmony shifted so she sat perfectly angled at the pianoforte, and though one eye was kept on the violinist so she knew when to begin, she tried desperately to look into the crowd for her sister.

There seemed to be half of Bath in the Pump Room that afternoon, and try as she might, she could not see Joy anywhere.

Someone cleared their throat, and Harmony's mind snapped back to the moment. The violinist was glaring at her.

Harmony blushed and placed her hands on the keys, exactly where they needed to be for this first movement.

Out of the corner of her eye, she could see Mr. Navarre, seated on her left, had raised his piccolo to his mouth. Everything about him seemed to move in a fluid motion, as if he had been born performing, born to create music, as if it were easier than breathing.

The violinist lifted his bow slightly, counted them in, and the music began.

The first few notes were the hardest. Harmony felt as though she was wading through water to get to them, and in a panic, she almost thought that she had picked the wrong sheet music.

But no. The clarinetist came in with a soft reedy counter-melody that reflected the glorious soaring of the violinist. The cello, strong and steady, followed the same route Harmony wandered down, her fingers feeling as though they were defrosting. The more she played, the more she realized something strange.

This was not difficult!

It was certainly a bizarre experience when someone in the Pump Room wandered a little more closely than she was accustomed to, but this was not hard.

In fact, this was easy!

Harmony's fingers soared across the keyboard, teasing out every dynamic of her music that perfectly resonated with the cello.

And then David Navarre began to play.

If Harmony had thought what they were playing before was music, there were no words for what they were playing now that he had joined in. Mr. Navarre coaxed his piccolo to create the most ethereal of sounds, sounds that Harmony had never heard before. It seemed impossible that he was creating such wonderful music with just a piccolo and nothing else, as if their music was earthly and his was angelic.

It was intoxicating, having him so close. As she reached for the lower ends of the pianoforte, Harmony almost felt as though she could reach out and touch him. As she came to a quieter part in her score, she turned her head ever so slightly to gain a better look at him—and gasped.

David Navarre was playing with his eyes closed and his heart on his sleeve, every ounce of passion poured through his instrument as though his life depended on it. The sharp line of his jaw was perfectly balanced and the intensity of music that he created made Harmony's heart flutter.

It did not hurt, of course, that he was far more handsome close up.

This was a man truly dedicated to his craft. The intensity of the experience almost made her want to forget playing herself, such an honor it was just to hear him in his element.

The cellist behind her coughed, loudly, and Harmony realized in horror she had missed her next entrance.

She was supposed to be playing, and now she had no idea where she was on the page!

Turning the score music with clammy hands, she quickly found her place and lowered her hands once more onto the keys. Face hot, she ensured she did not raise her eyes from the sheet music again, both to avoid any strange looks that their audience may shoot her way and to prevent herself from being distracted once more by the exhilarating David Navarre.

She would not let Monsieur Bernard down, nor herself.

The rest of the performance flew by. Before Harmony had time to even think, it was all over. Gentle applause rippled through the room, but in Harmony's eyes, it was nothing considering the mastery displayed by the musicians around her.

"I must congratulate you," said a low voice full of emotion.

David Navarre, panting slightly with exertion. Harmony flushed. He could not have been talking to her, surely.

"You have a true musician's talent," he said with a smile. "I knew I had not misjudged you."

"How can you say that?" Harmony whispered, unconsciously twisting to face him. "After what you have created, how can you even speak of my own playing?"

"Harmony!"

Mr. Navarre's response, whatever it was, was drowned out by Joy's shout across the room.

"Harmony! Harmony!"

Harmony glanced up to see her sister fighting through the crowd to reach her. The most unfortunate timing. Although she knew she should be glad a member of her family had actually witnessed it, for some reason she was irritated by Joy's decision to shout her name at that precise moment.

"I must say," said Joy when she finally reached them and leaned against the pianoforte, "I have never heard such music in all my life! And I say that as an expert, you know," looking around at the rest of the musicians, "for I am someone who has been dragged from pillar to post attending concerts against her will for nigh on a decade."

"That was beautiful, Harmony!" Esther joined her cousin, appearing from behind a group of gentlemen talking earnestly and seriously over a newspaper. Lucy was beside her.

Harmony let out the breath that she had not even realized she had been holding in.

"You came," she said in relief, a dazed smile on her face. "All three of you! Oh, thank you. What did you think?"

"Just incredible," said Lucy, "I am, as usual, in complete awe of your talents, Harmony."

"And I," Esther added, but she said nothing more. Instead, her gaze was fixed upon the gentleman standing beside her sister.

Harmony flushed. She herself was trying not to turn her head, determined not to see what expression David Navarre had on his face. She would not look, she would not look, she would not look…

Harmony looked. David Navarre was smiling.

"Miss Fitzroy," he said with an easy smile, rising from his seat and giving a deep bow to her family, "you have completely neglected to introduce me to these fine young ladies."

Jealously shot through Harmony like a thunderbolt—one so strong, she almost physically reeled from the shock.

She had never felt compared to Joy before, and when her myriad of cousins came to visit, they were always so different, their characters so unique, there was never any point in comparing them. One could draw, one was smart, another was beautiful; they were all exceptional women in their own way.

But as women, plain and simple, Harmony hated being grouped together.

The Fitzroys.

It lost her entirely. The quietest, the most likely not to speak out in a conversation, Harmony knew she was no stunning beauty and had no clever tricks to attract a man. Besides Joy, with her wit and cleverness, or Lucy, with her soft smile and gentle temper, there was really no point in her being there.

Someone coughed.

Harmony started. Mr. Navarre was staring at her, a little concern crinkling around his eyes. It was then she realized she had not replied.

"My apologies," said Harmony nervously. She stood up too quickly and crashed her knees against the pianoforte. "Miss Joy Fitzroy, Miss Esther Fitzroy, Miss Lucy Fitzroy. Mr. David Navarre."

Her sister and cousins curtseyed, and it was only now Harmony had the presence of mind to actually look at them.

Esther's hair was slightly ruffled by the stormy winds, but her white gown was thankfully free from any staining from snow—but really, thought Harmony, with her glorious ginger hair, Lucy's propensity to favor blue gowns was asking for attention. Joy had borrowed one of Harmony's dresses of a delicate topaz color that highlighted her golden hair beautifully.

If only they were not all so beautiful. If only Joy was not so witty, or Lucy so kind, or Esther so winning.

If only she could have David—Mr. Navarre, she must remember to call him Mr. Navarre—to herself.

Mr. Navarre smiled at the quartet, but Harmony thought for a moment that his smile was warmest when it was moving in her own direction.

You're a fool, she told herself severely. *You think a gentleman like that would spend any serious time thinking of you?*

"Dear ladies," he said, piccolo still in hand, "is it possible your parents have been so blessed four times over?"

"Fear not," said Joy quickly with a smile, "Harmony is my younger sister, and these are two of our cousins, visiting from London."

"I hope that your visit is turning out to be pleasant?" David Navarre looked primarily at Esther, as Lucy was struggling to keep her composure.

A smile tugged at his lips, and Harmony saw Lucy's giggles were not as well hidden as she clearly thought.

Harmony could not help but smile, for Mr. Navarre was evidently a true gentleman, or he would have mentioned it.

Esther responded politely, "Very pleasant indeed, Mr. Navarre, although the continuous snow does make it slightly more cumbersome for visiting in the afternoons."

"Which reminds me," cut in Joy, "we should be returning at once, or Father will be furious."

"Furious?" questioned Mr. Navarre, eyebrow raised.

"Not furious, as such," said Harmony quietly, "but my sister is right, I was only permitted to play today if we returned directly."

"Well then," said Mr. Navarre, "I shall only be two moments."

He sat down and began to place his piccolo back carefully and lovingly into its case.

Harmony watched him, his hands caressing the instrument. In an instant, she pictured what it would be to have those same hands caressing her. Touching her delicately and then with vigor. Bringing her hands to his lips and kissing her…

Someone nudged her, and Harmony felt her cheeks darken.

"Two moments?" Joy mouthed.

Harmony shrugged in reply. Her sister nodded her head toward him, and Harmony sighed.

"Mr. Navarre?"

He looked up at her words and gave her such a stunning smile she almost quite forgot what she was about to inquire of him.

"Mr. Navarre," Harmony began again, "may I ask what you mean by two moments?"

Looking slightly perplexed, Mr. Navarre gestured at his piccolo. "I shall not be long, I swear."

"No, you misunderstand me." Harmony sat back down on the stool for the pianoforte, her natural setting; she was amazed to feel so much more comfortable and confident there. "I meant, what will you be doing once those two moments will be over?"

"Why, accompanying you home, of course!" Mr. Navarre was gathering up the sheet music on his stand and putting them in the folder that was leaning against his chair. "I cannot have four beautiful young ladies such as yourselves return home alone, can I? It will be my pleasure," he said, the last words over Harmony's gentle protestations.

"But," said Harmony helplessly, but before she was able to say any more, Mr. Navarre had already packed away both music and piccolo and was putting on his greatcoat.

"Come on, Harmony," Esther whispered, "your pelisse, you will need to put it on as it is mightily cold outside."

Three minutes later, though Harmony had little understanding of exactly how, she found herself walking with Mr. Navarre a few steps behind Joy, Esther, and Lucy. It did not take long for her family to gain a lead, and before Harmony knew it, she and Mr. Navarre were talking in private.

"You did not tell me you had a close family," he remarked.

The wind was cold that afternoon, and the sun was already beginning to set, and he had his greatcoat turned up around the lapel.

Harmony laughed, then looked away from him. "You did not give me much of a chance to say anything, Mr. Navarre! One moment I was spying on you—for which I do apologize—the next I am accompanying you in a concert!"

Mr. Navarre's laughter sounded like honey. "I move and think quickly, I will admit!"

"And yet," said Harmony, meandering around a young gentleman who was determined not to move out of her path, so that her right-hand sleeve lightly brushed Mr. Navarre's, "in your playing you are so composed, so controlled—so free."

Mr. Navarre answered with a smile. "We are much alike in that regard, I think."

A blush of pleasure rippled across Harmony's face. She moved slightly to her left, increasing the distance between them as it originally was, but Mr. Navarre moved closer, bridging the gap and bringing their hands only a finger's breadth away.

"I am still a student in that regard," she said quietly.

"And I the master?"

Harmony laughed. "Very much so! You cannot comprehend what a delight it was to play with you, Mr. Navarre. You are so accomplished, it almost makes me ashamed of my own aptitude."

Joy had clearly just said something very amusing, for Esther and Lucy roared with laughter in unison. The two sisters were arm in arm, and Lucy had to lean on her sister to keep her balance. Harmony laughed in spite of herself.

"You are close, I think," remarked Mr. Navarre. "Your family."

Harmony shrugged, and with a spark of something she did not quite understand, her gloved fingers brushed against his. "As close as most sisters and cousins are, I would think."

"Much closer than I am with my brother."

There was a slight darkness in his voice, but Harmony ignored it. She was not one to pry into another's secrets.

Instead, she said, "I have no brothers. All I can say with any certainty is that I am fortunate indeed to have a genuine affection for my family members. In fact, I think I would wish to befriend them, even if they were not my flesh and blood."

They now turned onto the street where Harmony and her family lived, the Royal Crescent, and she found herself saddened that the journey had passed by so quickly.

Had they really walked all that way? She had barely noticed it.

"And here we are," she said quietly.

Joy, Esther, and Lucy reached the front door, and they pushed the door open to let themselves in. Mrs. Bird did not consider Bath a terribly dangerous place, Harmony knew, and only locked the doors at night.

Harmony stopped by the front step, and David Navarre mirrored her. It was only when he stood there, directly beside her, that she realized just how tall he was—a good head above her, and with a frame that was masculine and strong.

"Well," she said quietly, looking up with a smile. It was a hesitant smile, but she was in many ways amazed that she had managed that.

David Navarre was smiling, too, but his smile seemed more knowing than hers did.

"Well," he repeated slowly, his gaze flickering from her eyes down to her lips, and back again.

God forbid she manage to get through a single conversation with a handsome gentleman without saying something foolish!

"Thank you," she said softly, hoping to bring the conversation to a close without further embarrassing herself. "For walking us home, I mean."

Mr. Navarre said nothing. He just looked at her. Looked at her as though she was the most incredible and yet strange thing that he had ever seen.

Harmony felt his presence, breathed in a shallow breath as he shifted his feet to move closer to her.

They were only inches apart now, inches that could be breached by just one subtle movement by her. Or him. Or both of them.

Mr. Navarre raised his right hand to brush a leaf from her shoulder—and then he continued to lift that hand. The softest touch grazed across her cheek. Before Harmony knew what was happening, he was cupping her cheek, tilting her head up ever so slightly so she was staring him full in the face.

Those gray eyes, those gray bewitching eyes which had taken her by surprise when she had first seen them, were staring into her own so intently that Harmony felt her breath shortening, felt her pulse racing.

The smallest movement. David Navarre lowered his head, millimeter by millimeter. Harmony's arms were by her sides, but she had an irresistible urge to bring them up, to clasp a man that she had only met yesterday toward her, feeling rather than knowing where this crescendo was leading them.

Mr. Navarre paused when his lips were only three or four

inches away from hers, and all of this time, he had not taken his eyes from hers.

"Mr. Navarre?"

It was but a breath that Harmony had managed, and it blossomed out into the cold air like a flower.

He chuckled, and without changing his stance, whispered, "I think David would sound much better coming from your lips. Harmony."

Before Harmony could do anything, say anything, think anything—he released her and was striding away as she fell against her front door for support.

CHAPTER FOUR

EACH FOOTSTEP DAVID Navarre took created a beat as his boot met the icy snow, but he did not hear it.

His ears were full of Miss Harmony Fitzroy's voice, the way her fingers met the keys, the softness of her hesitation as she looked at him.

So entranced by his memories of her, he almost walked by his rooms in Camden Place.

Shaking his head, he retraced his steps and rapped smartly on the front door of his Bath lodgings—unlike the Fitzroys, David preferred a little more security in his home. It took only a moment for Rogers to reach the door.

"Good afternoon, sir," bowed Rogers, and David could not help but smile.

"No need for the bow, you know that," he said effortlessly, stepping past his butler. "And I must say, it still feels rather odd for you to address me as 'sir.'"

Rogers drew himself up stiffly. "Yes, sir."

David was too occupied shrugging off his greatcoat and dropping it, still soaking wet, on one of the embroidered chairs in the hallway. Six of them lined the space, but two were covered by other greatcoats that David had tried on that morning and decided that he did not want to wear. One had been turned inside out, and another was covered in inky musical notes annotated in a fine, strong hand.

"The study's got a fire, right Rogers?"

Rogers sighed, his gaze taking in the chaos his master always left in his wake. "Yes, sir."

David strode across the hallway, piccolo and sheet music bag in hand, opened the door, and moved through with Rogers in his wake.

Throwing himself in the leather armchair by the fire, David smiled with satisfaction, pulled off the strangling red necktie, and glanced around the room.

He'd had it redecorated when he had moved in, and it was now a perfect reflection of himself—strewn through with music and not much else.

It was clear Rogers had been in here, attempting to tidy up, but it was an impossible task. Sheet music covered every spare spot in the room, and David had the rather uncomfortable feeling he was sitting on some.

Rogers was standing to attention opposite him, his dark brown mustache quivering as if he was holding something very important back.

Which, David reminded himself, he almost certainly was. After all, Rogers was the man sent by *the company*.

"Sir," Rogers began stiffly, "it befalls me to mention to you, as it is approaching Christmas so swiftly, that your duties at the company have not waned and have, in fact, become more urgent. Just a short trip to Manchester would easily—"

"There'll be no trips to Manchester," David said curtly, throwing his legs over the arm of the armchair and shuffling to get comfortable. "So, you can forget about that, Rogers."

"But the company, sir." Rogers' voice was not pleading, as such, but was definitely concerted. "Their requirements of you are such that they simply cannot proceed in essential matters of business without—"

"Poppycock." David picked up the case that contained his piccolo from where he had carefully placed it beside the armchair on a small table and began to piece together his favorite instrument. "If Tristan cannot manage without me, that is his affair. He made it quite clear to me last time I saw him, that I was somewhat unnecessary to the family business. In fact, I seem to recall his words were distinctly direct about it. I think the term 'black sheep of the family' was used."

Rogers made a movement toward him, mouth open, but David raised up his piccolo with a sharp look.

"No, Rogers," he said firmly. "I know you were chosen by my brother and the company, and I have not complained because I have found you a rather endearing man to have around. But I will not brook further conversation on this."

"I only thought to mention," said Rogers with a downcast expression, "that since your wealth—your extreme wealth, if you do not mind me saying so, sir—has been derived from the company, perhaps—"

"My wealth," spat David. "Yes, I suppose you could call it that."

He brought his piccolo up to his chest and held it there for a moment. Wealth. Money. Gold coins, heavy ledgers, smiles when one entered the bank.

Tristan could keep it.

"My wealth, Rogers, was created by my father. A good man, a man who understood the real value of things, and since his death, my brother has seen fit to change a good many things which made our business great. Now, I may not have to work and may call myself a gentleman of leisure, and I am grateful for it." David took a deep breath. More grateful than his brother would ever know, but it was thanks to their father, not him. "But that does not excuse what my brother has done, and that gives me no debt of honor on his account. Now, wealth allows me to do what I love, and that is play music. And that is my only, and last, thought on the matter."

His gaze drifted toward the fireplace and alighted on some sheet music that had been stuffed rather unceremoniously between the fire tongs and the coal scuttle.

"Ah, Mozart," David said in a happier tone. He leaned forward, pulled it out from its partial hiding place, and laid it flat on the table beside him.

Rogers coughed slightly. "Would sir like me to run through his correspondence of today?"

"What?" Looking up, David shook his head slightly, surprised to see his butler still there. "Oh, of course, Rogers. Anything, as long as it does not originate from Manchester."

He smiled then, and his butler felt no compunction about smiling back. It was a strange person who was not, even in a small way, charmed by David Navarre.

"There were but two notes which came for you today, sir," said Rogers, bringing them out of his waistcoat pocket. "The first was sent by Mr. Bernard."

An Englishman to the core, Rogers did not bother to use a French accent, and David grinned at the Anglicization of his music teacher's name.

"Good news, I hope?"

"Indeed, sir," said Rogers, scanning the page. "It says here that everything is organized for the Christmas Eve concert at the Assembly Room for this year, and he is expecting you this coming Monday for your rehearsal."

"Excellent, excellent," murmured David, his eyes flickering between Rogers standing before him and the music of Mozart so tantalizingly before him. "And the other?"

Rogers could not help but puff out his chest as he read this one. "From the Contessa Giorgia, sir."

David was not a man who was easily impressed. "Hmm?"

Clearly disappointed by his master's lack of enthusiasm, Rogers wilted. "She asks that you and your pipers grant her the pleasure of playing at her party this Friday. She repeats twice what an honor it would be to have David Navarre playing in her home and emphasizes at the end that she is asking you and your ten pipers."

"Eleven pipers piping at a party?" David crinkled up his nose. "We are traditionally asked to play at gatherings in the outdoors, parades, that sort of thing. This is certainly a rather unusual request."

"If I may be so bold, sir," said Rogers, evidently going to continue regardless, "the contessa is well known in circles of both music and taste, and it would greatly improve your relationship with the aristocracy here in Bath if you were to be seen as patronized by her."

David shrugged. "It makes no difference to me, Rogers, whether the aristocracy like me or not."

"Nevertheless," Rogers said firmly, "it can only benefit you, sir, if you are seen in the presence of such people. It will cost you but an evening with your pipers, and I had thought it would be something that you would enjoy."

There were few butlers in the world who could be so direct, but David was so uninterested in decorum that he barely noticed when Rogers overstepped the line.

Stretching out his hand to pick up the music by Mozart, David sighed. "Very well, Rogers, have it your way. Send a note to each of my pipers, tell them the time and place. Instruct them that we shall play the usual, dress code is Court Dress."

Rogers bowed and turned to leave the room, but he hesitated at the door.

"Yes?"

Rogers coughed. "Am I required to respond to the invitation from the contessa, to verify that the eleven pipers will be attending?"

David nodded absentmindedly, then said quickly, "Wait, Rogers."

It was a rather wild idea, but then why not? He hardly ever used his name to do anything he wanted. Why not this?

"Tell her I have one condition for our attendance." He smiled, despite himself, as he watched Rogers brace himself. "Tell her David Navarre and his pipers will be happy to play for her this

Friday, as long as the family of Mr. Rupert Fitzroy, of the Royal Crescent, is also in attendance."

THE FIRST THING Harmony noticed when she stepped from the frozen street into the large and overwhelmingly grand hallway she had never been in before was the sound.

That is, the melee of sounds: chatter coming through a doorway, which showed card tables; the heavy steps of couples dancing in what could only be the ballroom to her left. There were people gathered about the hallway, gossip flying from tongue to tongue, and the music—the sheer splendor of the music almost knocked her over.

"Careful, Harmony!" Joy hissed. "You stood on my foot!"

Harmony opened her mouth to utter an apology, but none came.

The second thing Harmony noticed was that she, her sister, and her cousins were miserably out of place.

The sweeping staircase in the hallway was covered with a luxurious red carpet, gold gilding on the banister, and directly above it was the largest chandelier she had ever seen. Paintings surrounded by large golden frames depicted family members stretching back hundreds of years, all of them looked very serious, and most of them included dogs or horses.

Everywhere Harmony looked, she saw wealth and grandeur and splendor.

"And you truly have no idea why we have been invited?" Esther spoke low, and Harmony could tell that she felt just as uncomfortable as she did to be standing in the hallway of a contessa.

Esther was usually so confident, it was unnerving for Harmony to see her so unsettled. She was even picking unconsciously at her pristine white gown, the silver stitching around the sleeves added purposefully for this very event.

Harmony shrugged helplessly. "I have no idea."

Esther's curiosity grew. "The invitation just…arrived?"

"That's all I know," said Rupert Fitzroy grandly. "Now your mother," and here he looked at his daughters, "has chosen to absent herself as her novel has reached, I am wisely informed, a most gripping part, I give you my leave to do whatsoever you wish. I would highly recommend a glass of punch and one glass only from the room to our right, if the raucous laughter is anything to go by, and I beg of you—no dancing with the same gentleman twice, any of you, or I shall have to suffer the expense of a wedding."

As Rupert strode toward the card tables, Lucy could not help but giggle.

"There is no one quite like your father, is there?" she said with a smile of wonder, a slightly shaking hand smoothing down the skirts of her cobalt blue silk gown. "I mean, there is not another father in the world who would give orders as he does!"

Joy rolled her eyes. "Whether that is our blessing or our curse is yet to be established. At any rate, let us move out of the way— we are clogging up the door!"

Harmony turned and saw that as she, Joy, Esther, and Lucy were all gathered right by the entrance, there was now a queue of ruffled people in very elegant cloaks behind them.

Moving further into the hallway, the four Fitzroys removed their cloaks and gave them to the footmen standing obligingly for that very use.

Harmony could now see that Joy had decided to wear her very favorite gown, a sapphire blue that truly made her tresses appear as fine gold curled around her head.

"What acquaintance do you have with the contessa?" Esther asked. "I am determined to find a logical explanation for this. Does your mother know her?"

"You would have a better chance of answering that question yourself," retorted Joy. "All I know of her is that she is a great admirer of music, a leading lady of fashion, and her primary residence is in London. Your part of the world."

"You truly do not know her?" Lucy sounded almost disappointed. "I was sure one of you must have met her daughter, or once danced with her son, or something, and gained an invitation through that means."

Joy shrugged. "Not I, I can assure you."

It took Harmony a moment to realize they were looking at her.

"Me?" She stuttered, then took a long deep breath to compose herself.

Just because she had never seen so much of the nobility and aristocracy in one place did not mean that she was going to lose all control of her faculties.

"Does Contessa Giorgia even have a daughter?" she asked in a slightly calmer voice. "I have not heard of one. You certainly cannot give me the praise of eliciting the invitation!"

"Miss Harmony Fitzroy!"

Harmony twirled on the spot and almost lost her balance for the second time in five minutes.

It was David Navarre.

Dressed in the most fashionable of styles, his breeches were fitted, and his coat had the high lapels that every gentleman of good standing was requesting from his tailor. Harmony could see he had not bothered to shave, leaving him instead with the stubble she was beginning to suspect was his preferred look. He had emerged from the ballroom, and it was only then that Harmony realized that the exquisite music had stopped.

"Is that…?"

Harmony had never heard her sister so shocked. "Yes," she said breathlessly. "It is."

He had been standing in the doorway to the ballroom but was now walking slowly towards them.

Mr. Navarre bowed before them. "I had not thought to gain the pleasure of your company this early in the evening, Miss

Harmony, yet here you are!"

He was speaking to her.

David Navarre. The most handsome man she had ever met. The most enticing. The most talented musician.

A man who, she was sure, would have kissed her on the doorstep a few days ago if only he had wanted to. Why hadn't he? Didn't he want to? But then why had he stood there looking at her like…like he wanted to take all her clothes off?

Harmony blinked. She had become lost in her thoughts, her cousins and sister staring at her—not to mention that David Navarre was still waiting for a response.

"Oh," she said hurriedly. "Thank you, Mr. Navarre!"

"Nothing could give me more pleasure," he said easily. "And it is good to see the entire Bath contingent of the Fitzroy clan out in force!"

Esther had the presence of mind to curtsey, but Lucy just stared. Harmony wished she would not. She had only just had the thought when Joy stood very purposefully on Lucy's foot. The resulting squeal gave Harmony time to gather her thoughts.

"It is so good to see a familiar face," Harmony said, smiling shyly. "We were unsure as to whether there would be anyone else from our acquaintance. Though I hope we have not taken you from your party."

"I see."

Mr. Navarre's face had fallen.

Though it was true she had hardly been able to stop thinking about that heart-stopping moment when he had reached up his hand and caressed her cheek, Harmony had no clarity of mind over what it had meant.

What did he want, this musician who seemed to be able to stare right into her soul with those gray eyes?

"I was hoping," said Harmony, testing out the waters, "that I would have the pleasure of seeing you dance, Mr. Navarre, but I am guessing by the current lack of it that you are responsible for the music that we were only just enjoying?"

"You are correct!" He grinned. "In fact, I think this is the first time you have seen my eleven pipers piping—come through, do!"

Before Harmony had a moment to think, Mr. Navarre had taken her left hand and was walking toward the ballroom.

It was incredible, the tingling feeling his touch created, even through their gloves. Harmony's fingers were so used to delicacy, especially when playing the pianoforte, but this was a feeling far beyond anything she had ever experienced.

"You see?"

Harmony stared wide-eyed at the ballroom. It had clearly been modeled on the Bath Assembly Rooms—or, as Harmony reminded herself, much more likely, the Bath Assembly Rooms were modeled on the Contessa Giorgia's ballroom.

There were no fewer than six chandeliers suspended from the ceiling, and their glittering candles were, in turn, reflected in the large mirrors along the walls, light glinting and sparkling everywhere.

The floor had been polished to brilliance, and the walls were painted to the latest designs—pastel green, with delicate paintwork in a darker shade to give it a subtle depth. The entire ballroom was immaculate, far more fashionable than any Harmony had seen.

But despite all the beauty, stunning architecture, and tasteful furnishings the contessa undoubtedly took great pride in, there was only one part of the ballroom that caught Harmony's attention.

"My word," she said breathlessly, "when you said pipers, I did not comprehend!"

David Navarre grinned, giving him an almost boyish appearance. "My eleven pipers piping!" he said proudly. "Of course, it really is only eleven when I am up there, but my ten piper players have all been handpicked by myself and play at the highest standard."

Harmony could not help but stare. On the stage area reserved for the musicians, instead of the typical stringed ensemble, there was a group of men, all holding piccolos and chatting and laughing with each other.

"But," said Harmony, turning to David—Mr. Navarre—excitedly, not noticing her fingers were still entwined with his own, "a piccolo ensemble?"

"A piccolo choir," he replied with a smile. "Isn't it marvelous? I have always adored the incredible singing sound that the piccolo can create, a sound like nothing else that you can experience, and so I thought—why not?"

Harmony laughed. "Did it never occur to you, Mr. Navarre—"

"David," he corrected gently. "I would prefer you to call me David when we are alone."

It was only then that Harmony realized her sister and cousins had not followed her; they were elsewhere in the ballroom, near the opposite side of the room, with punch glasses in hand.

Hands.

The proximity of David Navarre was now almost unbearably apparent now, and the feeling of his fingers gathered in with hers…

"Do not concern yourself," said David quietly as though able to hear her thoughts. "I did not intend to separate you from your family. I have no harmful intentions, I promise you."

"I know," said Harmony, smiling at him—and when she said the words out loud did she know he could never hurt her. It was not in him. No one who played such beautiful music could even consider something harmful. Besides, he…he made her feel safe. "'Tis just that—"

"We met less than a week ago," finished David with a knowing smile.

Harmony smiled despite herself. "Well, yes! Do you not find it strange that you wish me to address you in such an informal manner? In such an," and here she had to swallow, "intimate way?"

There was movement all around them, but Harmony hardly noticed it. What care she for ladies and gentlemen she did not know?

David's smile faded, but he did not appear angry or upset with her. Quite to the contrary. His expression changed to that look of intensity he'd had when he had walked her home.

That afternoon when he had been sure he would kiss her. Had wanted him to. Had wondered where this fire within her had sprung from.

"Mr. Navarre," she said quietly. When he took a small step toward her, expression unchanged but for the hint of a smile, Harmony tried again. "David!"

He stopped. Harmony could hear rushing in her ears, as if she was standing underneath a waterfall, and she could not drag her gaze away from his face. They seemed moments away from something unheard of, something unfathomable, something truly wonderful.

"Harmony," said David Navarre in a jagged whisper, "I—"

"Navarre!" A man Harmony recognized as one of the pipers knocked her shoulder as he pushed through the crowds to reach them. The moment between her and David, whatever it was, whatever it could have been, was broken. "Are you coming to lead us, or not?"

David breathed a heavy sigh and dropped his head for a moment. Harmony could feel his frustration, shared it.

Perhaps standing in the middle of a ballroom at a large private party was not the best place for an intimate moment.

Harmony squeezed his hand. "David," she said softly, "this conversation is not over, it is just paused. For now."

Soulful gray eyes looked into hers, and he gave her that smile that already had the power to melt her insides.

Raising her hand, David pressed her white glove to his lips. "I will hold you to that."

CHAPTER FIVE

"A RE YOU SURE you will not come with us, Harmony? Harmony!"

Harmony jerked up her head and looked round, startled. "What?"

Joy tutted. She and Esther were dressed in matching Spencer jackets, cream with gold beading around the hems. Joy had favored her beautiful ruby gown, with a bonnet made from the same material, and Esther had departed—at least for today—from her favorite white and had chosen a cream gown.

Their journey to the Pump Rooms was without Lucy, who, to her own irritation, had fallen sick with a cold—caught, Harmony was sure, from the crush around the punch bowl at the contessa's, three days before.

"I said," Joy repeated, just a hint of impatience running through her voice, "are you sure won't come with us? It does you no good being holed up with your pianoforte all day. You'll make yourself ill!"

"No, I won't," Harmony spoke almost automatically. In truth, her shoulders ached from sitting over the pianoforte since the early hours, and she had not been sleeping at all well since the Contessa Giorgia's ball.

Every time she closed her eyes, she saw not darkness but a gray—the same gray that graced David Navarre's eyes.

When she tried to sleep, all she could hear was the captivating music the eleven pipers piping wove through the air. Every time she ate, she was reminded of the small pastries served by elegant footmen and the look David had sent searing in her direction.

He had been talking to the contessa, yet as Harmony had watched him, his attention drifted, and he had looked right over the contessa's shoulder, straight at her.

Every moment away from him just seemed to be an interlude before she could see him again.

"Harmony!"

This time it was Esther whose voice sounded frayed, and Harmony jerked to attention, her gaze lifting from the repeated print pattern on her rose-pink gown.

"My apologies, Esther," she said frankly. "I am afraid my mind is not really here. I would be ill company in the Pump Rooms. I am best left on my own. I will work this through my system, and I shall be as right as rain when you return."

Esther and Joy exchanged a look.

"'Tis just nerves," Harmony said quietly. "You know I am not…well, not the most forward character—I don't have your confidence, Esther, or your wit, Joy. I have only performed once in public before, and you heard the mistakes I made!"

Esther sat in the chair Harmony had behind her pianoforte stool, there for Monsieur Bernard anytime they had her music lesson at the Fitzroys'.

"Harmony," said Esther, "you made one mistake in that performance, and as you say it was the first time you had ever performed—and I am sure the majority of people there that day did not even notice."

"Joy did," Harmony said with a wry smile, "I know it."

"Well of course I did," said Joy, shaking her head with a smile. "I had heard you play that music from dawn that very morning, over and over! I should be a dullard indeed if I had forgotten it by the time I had walked from here to there!"

Harmony laughed, despite herself. "I did not think about it in that way, I must confess. Do you honestly think that it went unnoticed?"

"I don't even think that the clarinetist noticed," said Joy in her usual frankness. "I would not concern yourself, Harmony. Not only will you excel in this Christmas Eve concert of yours, but you may find yourself in demand in the New Year!"

Both she and Esther laughed, and Harmony joined them. "You always know just what to say," she said gratefully. "Thank you."

"Nonsense," Joy was brisk, and she tapped Esther's shoulder. "Honesty is the best policy, I always say. Now come, Esther—at this rate, there will be no point in us going at all!"

The house fell into its usual quiet as the front door slammed. Harmony luxuriated in the silence of it all; the only time she felt truly comfortable practicing, even now, was when as far as she could hear, the house was empty.

But this feeling did not help her today.

The Christmas Eve concert is only two weeks away, Harmony thought desperately as her fingers became entangled at the end of a particularly difficult page, *and I am no closer to getting to the bottom of this phrasing than I was yesterday.*

The primary difficulty, Harmony admitted to herself, was that each time one of her slender fingers touched a key, all she could think about was the warmth through her gloves when David had held her hand. Every time she played a note, she heard not the pianoforte's tone but the song of a piccolo and David's piping choir.

Harmony shook her head and arms, the rose-pink sleeves pushed up to her elbows, then laid her hands onto the keys. She was not going to get distracted by David Navarre.

David Navarre. The man who was standing outside the window, waving to get her attention!

"David," she whispered, and as if he could read her lips, he treated her to a wide smile. Gaining courage, Harmony said in a stronger voice, "David, what are you doing here?"

It was only when David's mouth moved that she realized she could not hear him.

"Go to the door," she gestured toward the front door. David nodded and disappeared from sight.

Harmony lifted her skirts and ran to the front door—the last thing that she wanted was for Mrs. Bird to open the door and find a strange young man there!

Scampering into the hallway, she heard one gentle knock before she was able to undo the latch and wrench the door open.

"My, what a sight for sore eyes!" There could not be a larger smile on David's face. "Harmony Fitzroy, I have missed you."

"David," said Harmony in a hiss, "what are you doing here?"

David blinked, confused. "Visiting you, of course."

"But you can't," Harmony said weakly. "I mean, we are barely acquainted, and I do not believe you have even met my father!"

It all seemed madness that such a gentleman could be standing on the doorstep. Her doorstep. There to see her! This was the sort of thing that happened to other people, not to her.

Snow was beginning to fall, and although David was wearing a greatcoat, she could see that he was starting to shiver.

"Are you really going to deny me entry?" he asked, a smile dancing around his lips.

Harmony shook her head slowly. "No. No, I'm not. Do come in, Mr. Navarre."

He raised an eyebrow before he entered, but obeyed her, nonetheless. Harmony closed the door behind him and leaned on it, staring at the man before her as if he were a wild animal: uncontained, unpredictable, and standing in her hallway.

David Navarre was in her home. Alone, with her.

"Your home really is beautiful," said David, swiveling on the spot to look around, pulling off his greatcoat as he went. Without really looking, he hung his coat on a hook on the wall, revealing impeccable taste in clothes once again if not manners. His dark hair appeared wilder than normal. "Where's your instrument?"

Absolutely no words came to Harmony to protest at the unusual circumstances of his arrival. He had not been invited, he did not know her father, and now he wished to see her pianoforte?

She swallowed. This was it. This was the sort of adventure other young ladies had, and she had always wondered what it would be to be pursued by a man.

Any man.

And here she was. She needed to grasp the opportunity with both hands.

Taking a deep breath, Harmony focused on the one anchor in this storm that David Navarre always brought with him: music.

"Through here," she said, her confidence growing the closer she moved toward her pianoforte.

David followed her, and Harmony heard his breath catch when he caught sight of it.

"My word, Harmony," he said, rushing toward it and running a worshipful hand over the keys, "you really do keep this beauty in good condition, if the outside is anything to go by."

"It is something that I am very particular on," said Harmony, closing the door to the music room and slipping onto the pianoforte seat. "I will admit, it is rather strange to have you here. My pianoforte is not something I am very good at sharing."

David paused and looked up at her with a smile. "I know exactly what you mean. Your instrument…it is a part of your soul, an extension of your very being."

"I quite agree," said another voice.

Both Harmony and David turned to the doorway, and Harmony blushed, despite willing herself not to, to see her father standing in the doorway.

What would her father say to find her alone with a gentleman?

But David did not seem unsettled at all. "Mr. Fitzroy, I presume? Such an honor to finally meet you," he said, striding over and bowing deeply.

Her father returned his civility, and though his face was all politeness, Harmony could see his smile did not extend to his eyes. "And it is splendid to meet you, young man, though I regret to say I have absolutely no idea who you are or what you are doing here."

"Papa," Harmony rose from her chair but did not seem to have the ability to walk forward, "this is Mr. David Navarre. He is a musician, we played together in the afternoon concert in the Pump Rooms that I was invited to by Monsieur Bernard."

"Who is the same person who has sent me hither this very day," said David, casting a smile to Harmony before he turned back to face her father. "Monsieur Bernard informed me Miss Fitzroy was desirous of additional music lessons, before the Christmas Eve concert, of course, and so he instructed me to come here."

Her father looked over the man before him and made a decision. "Excellent. I thank you, Mr. Navarre, for the time you will be dedicating to my daughter's study—I know the musician's lot is not an easy one, and there is little money in it, but I hope you are receiving the honor it affords."

Harmony flushed. To think that her own father would mention money—and to a complete stranger! He had never been one to follow decorum and society's ideas of manners, but to bring up such a distasteful and private subject with a man that you had only just learned the name of; it was more than she had ever expected from him.

Her eyes turned to David. Surely now he had been so offended, it would take him but minutes to politely make his excuses and depart. After all, there was no chance Monsieur Bernard had actually asked him to come here.

"Sir, I receive more honor and pleasure from teaching my pupils and imparting my musical experience than I do performing," replied David smoothly, his smile broadening.

This had clearly not been the response her father had been expecting.

"Well, then," he said uncertainly. "Good. Excellent. I shall leave you to it then. Will you be joining us for luncheon, Mr. Navarre?"

Despite herself, despite her better judgment, Harmony hoped silently he would accept. To spend more time with him—more importantly, to see him with her family…

But she was getting ahead of herself. Foolish woman! Harmony tried desperately to remind herself that David was not here to court her, surely. He was here…perhaps out of curiosity.

He would not be wishing to spend time with her family.

And he proved her right.

But David sighed. "Alas, I simply cannot, Mr. Fitzroy, but I greatly appreciate the offer. Perhaps another time?"

Her father nodded. "Perhaps."

The two men exchanged bows, and David and Harmony were left alone. The music room door closed quietly with a snap.

Harmony let the silence settle and stared at David. "You must allow me to apologize on behalf of my father, Mr. Navarre—"

"David," he corrected, almost automatically, "and why? I like your father, he is a forthright man. I know where I stand with him."

"But to mention…to refer to your finances," said Harmony, trying to hide her mortification for bringing it up herself. "I cannot apologize enough."

David shrugged. "It does not concern me. Take heed, Harmony. I do not want you to ever be afraid of speaking to me on any subject. Any subject whatsoever, understand?"

Harmony nodded. It was not possible for her at this moment to reply with actual words, her shyness overwhelming her as she knew it would.

Speak to him on any subject. David, to her.

It was all too much. It was far more intimate than was appropriate, and yet it felt so right. She was drawn to him, inexorably, and he did not appear to wish to keep her at a distance.

Perhaps he did desire her. Harmony's gaze trailed over his

lips, that sharp jawline, the way his eyes seemed to sparkle as he looked at her.

Did he wish to touch her as she wished to touch him? What would his fingertips feel like along the curve of her cheek, this time not departing but remaining until he kissed her, his mouth—

"Harmony? Can you hear me?"

Harmony flushed. David was staring at her, concerned. She needed to pay attention!

"Why did you say Monsieur Bernard sent you here?" She asked, trying not to sound as though she was accusing him, but failing. "That is not true, is it?"

David's jaw dropped. "How in God's name...pardon me, Harmony, but how did you catch me in a falsehood?"

Harmony could not help but smile, and it broadened when she saw just how perplexed she had made him.

"No, I ask in earnest!" David moved toward her, but warily now, as if she were an unknown creature. "You are the one who is constantly reminding me we have not been acquainted long, yet you caught me in a lie which some of my closest friends could not have discerned."

Harmony shrugged and tried to keep her composure. She must not see too much into this. "I think I know enough of you, even by now, to know you are a man quite prepared to decide to come and visit me, excuse or nay."

David's gray eyes danced, and he chuckled as he said, "I may have unknowingly underestimated you before, Harmony, but I shall not do so again."

Without her even noticing, David had moved closer, until they were almost touching.

"You had better not," whispered Harmony shyly and was rewarded with another wry smile from the handsome man before her.

The moment held, undisturbed. Harmony was hanging in the air like a puppet, unable to pull her own strings, unable to move away from him.

Not that she wanted to. A day that had started gray, cold, and damp, both outside in the street and within her own ability to play, was now becoming something quite different.

"Now," said David softly, his throat sounding dry, "what were you practicing?"

It took a moment for Harmony to comprehend to what he was referring.

"Music," she said softly, not taking her eyes from his.

She knew she had to reply, but she wanted more than anything else for this moment, whatever they were sharing, to continue forever.

David blinked. "Any particular composer?"

He took a slight step backward as he spoke, and Harmony was obliged to shake her head slightly, as if she had newly emerged from water.

They had to be careful. Whatever that was, whatever this was between them, she could not control herself around him. The last thing the Fitzroy family needed was a scandal, now Cousin Caroline had become engaged.

"Handel," she said, a little more strength in her voice. "Part of the Water Music—you know it, of course."

"Know it?" David settled himself on the seat behind the pianoforte stool and smiled up at her. "I have written four different arrangements, one of which my eleven pipers piping find most enjoyable—as do our audiences. Or at least," he said with a wry smile, "that is what they tell me."

Harmony moved to her instrument, sat, and moved the music sheets to the beginning. "I wish I knew it so well. It is a piece of music I have only heard performed twice, yet it captured my imagination in a way few other pieces have."

Harmony had expected David to respond; she could see him slightly in her peripheral vision, just out of the corner of her right eye. When he did not, she turned her head and saw that he had fixed her with a deeply emotional gaze.

"Mr. Nav...David?"

David sighed, his smile softening. "I'm sorry, Harmony. I never thought I would meet another person who shared my love of music in the visceral, the very physical way you do. Let alone a young lady of such beauty."

Harmony colored, pushing an errant strand of hair behind her ear self-consciously. "Joy is the beauty of the family," she said awkwardly. "But...I thank you."

David shook his head. "Harmony Fitzroy, I never know how to proceed with you! Each time I consider myself to have mastered your character, you surprise me. Is it truly possible you have no idea how captivating you look?"

"David, you jest—and you are embarrassing me," protested Harmony.

"I do not jest."

Harmony's nervous smile disappeared. "You...you do not?"

For an instant, Harmony genuinely thought he was going to lean forward and kiss her. He shifted, certainly, and in her direction—but something held him back. Though there was desire there, and she could no longer mistake it for anything else, something restrained him.

"Music," he said finally, his eyes flickering over her face. "Let's get you playing, and we can see what is happening."

Harmony blinked. "I thought helping me with the music was just an excuse to...to I know not what, if I am frank."

And she was. Somehow, she was able to be honest with David in a way that surprised her. Words she would have only thought with others were spoken to him. Harmony did not understand.

"Neither do I," mused David, not breaking her gaze and answering the question she had asked in the privacy of her own mind. "Yet here I am. Now play."

Harmony was tempted to ask him again, to inquire exactly what he was doing at her home, in the music room, seated not five inches behind her—and yet her eagerness to gain his opinion on her performance was stronger.

She turned, breathed, placed her fingers on the keys, and began.

Within moments, Harmony had completely forgotten there was anyone else in the room. Her hands sprang to life as if they had been rested for hours, not minutes, and the complexity of the music was this time conquered by her dexterous fingers.

It was not until she reached a particularly difficult part that she stumbled, and she immediately drew herself to a halt.

"Blast it to hell," she muttered—and then swiveled round, mortified.

Goodness! So accustomed was she to being in the music room alone when she practiced, she had slipped into some terribly bad habits. Her mother would faint to hear her use such language!

"Good God, Harmony, I certainly feel less shamed about my previous outburst! Where did you learn language like that?"

Harmony smiled weakly. "Where anyone learns it, I suppose, from the people around them. It is almost impossible to walk anywhere in Bath without hearing such language, though I always reserve it for when I am alone."

"You're not alone now," said David quietly.

Every word which came out of his mouth dripped with honey, and Harmony knew it was becoming ever more difficult to be so close to someone so—attractive was not the right word.

David was handsome, certainly, with the looks many gentlemen would kill for, but there was something else about him.

Harmony felt...drawn to him, that was the only way she could describe it. As though she was being pulled toward him like the magnetic lodestones she had once seen a blacksmith use to remove iron filings.

David seemed completely inescapable, and she had never been so glad of anything in her life.

"...the phrase on the second page."

David was talking, and Harmony—so lost in her thoughts—had not been paying any attention whatsoever. She turned hurriedly and scrambled to find the phrase he was speaking of.

"Yes, there," he said, moving his seat to place it directly behind her.

Harmony tried to turn. "David, what are you doing?"

"Trust me," he said evenly.

Hesitating only a moment, Harmony faced her pianoforte once again. She waited there for a moment, unsure what was to happen. She heard a strange rustling sound of fabric, and then she gasped.

Hands had appeared on either side of her, attached to arms whose shirtsleeves had been rolled up. Harmony could see their strength, the muscle that twisted as he moved. David's arms. David's arms around her. She was encircled in him and could now feel the heat of his chest behind her.

Gently, he closed the gap. Harmony swallowed as she felt his heartbeat in her back. This was…this was more than she could have ever imagined. This was scandalous. This was wild.

This was exactly what she wanted.

"David," she whispered, shocked at how shaky her voice was. "David, what—"

"Do not concern yourself," David's voice breathed in her left ear, his warmth on her neck. "Watch."

Harmony tried to watch, but she was unable to control her breathing as his hands moved firmly over the keys. Lovingly.

David swallowed, echoing in Harmony's ears. "First page, please."

She raised her hands to organize the music and leaned back—just to feel herself nestled in the strength of David's chest.

"David—"

"Listen," urged David. Then he began to play.

Harmony could have sat there for hours. The warmth of his body, the feeling of his hands moving across her pianoforte, the sturdy arms encircling her, the music that pervaded her dreams surrounding her…she would never experience anything like this again.

"You see?" David's voice was low and deep. Harmony could feel his breath on the back of her neck. "The phrasing is altered, listen."

Harmony tried to listen, but she was more aware that her breathing had settled into the same rhythm as his. It was as if they were one person, one body, one soul.

"Harmony?"

She could not help it. Harmony relaxed into his arms, giving herself up to the bliss of being there. She heard David sigh contentedly, and then she felt something warm and soft brush the side of her neck.

The music slowed, his arms became more sluggish, his fingers dawdling across the keys.

A kiss. Her first, and not on her lips, but instead in that delicate spot just below her left ear. Her entire body shivered with the intensity of it, the intimacy of it all.

David Navarre was kissing her.

"David," she breathed.

He did not reply. At least, not in words. Harmony felt his lips lower once more to her neck, and this time the kiss was stronger, firmer, more certain. The stubble she had looked at so often grazed her skin, and she reveled in it. Her eyes fluttered shut, so that she did not see but instead felt his hands leave the keys and gently place themselves on her waist.

"David," she murmured, without any idea what she was going to say—or what he would say.

But he did not need words to express how he felt at this moment.

The scratch of his stubble raked across her neck, and she could bear it no longer. She moved instinctively, trying to turn.

"Harmony," he murmured under his breath as Harmony turned to face him.

Her eyes were open now, and she could drink in every element of this moment, the way his gray eyes were staring at her with such hunger, such longing.

This was the moment she would retreat. This was not the sort of thing that happened to Harmony Fitzroy!

She swallowed. It was happening—and she wanted more.

Harmony leaned forward, bridging the gap between them, and brushed her lips over his.

The moan David let forth told her she had been right, that he wanted her to kiss him just as much as she had wanted to.

Before Harmony knew what was happening, David had pulled her to her feet, and once again his strong arms were around her, gentle yet firm. Harmony's eyes were closed, and all she could do was marvel at the softness and the warmth of his lips, the way he had tilted his jaw against hers, the tingle jumping through her body from her head to her toes. The symphony that they were creating together was one she wanted to play for the rest of her life.

She did not want the moment to end but end it did.

"Harmony?"

The voice came from the hallway.

Harmony thought David would jump away from her, but instead, he broke the kiss and looked at her, raising a hand from her waist up to her face, stroking it, pushing a strand of hair behind her ear.

"Harmony," he murmured. "Dear God. I have wanted to do that from the first moment I saw you."

"I know," Harmony found herself breathing. "I wanted you to."

They stood there for a heart-shattering moment, so close to an intimacy Harmony knew was forbidden, yet only a door stood between them and scandal.

"Harmony, where are you?"

"That is Lucy," Harmony whispered weakly. "She is unwell, I must go to her."

"I very much enjoyed this music lesson, Harmony Fitzroy," David said with a wry smile. "And I would like to repeat it as soon as possible."

"Harmony?"

Lucy's voice was plaintive and seemed to be getting closer—but David clearly had no intention of letting Harmony go just yet. His hands still encircled her waist, each finger a searing promise of something more to come.

"Tomorrow," said Harmony quietly. "The Lower Rooms."

"Two in the afternoon would suit, though I am loath to leave you."

"Tomorrow," repeated Harmony with a smile. "You will not have too long to wait."

David sighed and released her. "Tomorrow. Too damn long."

CHAPTER SIX

FOR THE FIRST time in his life, David sat for hours in the study with his piccolo in his lap and not to his lips.

A coal shifted in the grate of the fire he always demanded was kept lit. He had sat for above an hour after picking at his breakfast, a robe thrown over the nightgown from which he had not bothered to change. Dark curls topped it at his neck; his bare feet were nestled in the long pile of the rug.

A knock at the door was the only thing able to penetrate his thoughts.

"Sir?" Rogers opened the door, unaccustomed to having his knocks unanswered.

David sighed. "Come in Rogers, what is it?"

Rogers did not exactly shuffle but seemed reticent to enter.

"Out with it, man." David's voice was not curt, but his temper was certainly frayed.

"Another letter from Manchester, sir, and I really think that this is one you should take a look at." Rogers did not look weary, as such, but as though he knew precisely how this conversation would play out.

"Hand it over," said David lazily.

Rogers offered the letter, unopened and with "Urgent" scrawled across it in large letters. The tiniest of movements was enough to throw it into the flames.

"Sir," said Rogers reproachfully, "you know full well, as I do, that your brother will not stop sending you these letters just because they go unanswered."

"On the contrary," said David swiftly, "I very much expect these letters will stop as soon as he starts to comprehend that he cannot have my money, my good wishes, or my guidance in caring for the company he stole from me."

"Your father's will was very specific," countered Rogers. "He gave his fortune to you, and the business to your brother—"

"Yes," spat David, trying to force down the bitterness. This was not who he was. "What a brilliant idea that was."

"—his intention," continued Rogers doggedly, "was that the two of you would be forced, finally, after all these years, to work together. I knew your father much longer than you, if you beg my impertinence, sir."

David glared at Rogers, who stood stoically under his gaze. It was fortunate for Rogers, thought David, that he had been such a constant presence of calm in his childhood. Otherwise, he would have found it much simpler just to remove him.

The grandfather clock in one corner of the room chimed one o'clock, and David's head shot over to it.

"I cannot talk about this now," said David abruptly, rising from his chair. "I have an urgent appointment to attend."

Rogers raised an inquiring eyebrow. "With a Miss Harmony Fitzroy, per chance?"

David stared at his butler. "How in God's name did you know that?"

"You underestimate the dialogue people entertain here in Bath," said Rogers, turning to walk out of the room—but David was not going to let him get away with that.

Following him into the hallway, he forced the butler to halt. "I'm serious, Rogers, that meeting was intended to be, to all intents and purposes, private. Are you saying there is gossip here about Harmony and myself?"

"I beg your pardon, sir," he said slowly, "but I had no idea you and—Miss Fitzroy, is it?—were so well acquainted."

David shook his head irritably. "What difference does it make? I ask you, how did you know of this?"

This was not ideal. He knew even the merest hint of scandal could ruin a lady's reputation, but he had not expected news to move so fast. It had been but twenty-four hours since he had…

David swallowed. God, he had only kissed her. How desperately he had wished to do more. Place Harmony on the keys and wrap her legs around him as he poured his passion onto her lips as she gasped in his mouth that—

"I would not concern yourself, sir," said Roger smoothly. "My knowledge is of an indirect kind and does not reflect badly on either you or the lady. I was approached by a young fellow, a Martin Seyton, who had been sent by a Mrs. Bird, who in turn had been requested by her employer, a Mr. Fitzroy."

"Goodness," said David, eyes wide, "I had no idea the world worked in such a way."

"You have no idea, sir." Rogers's voice was dry, but he smiled. "In any case, the question put to me by young Seyton was whether or not you, sir, had a suitable income to support yourself. Or perhaps, a wife."

"By God!" burst out David. "What kind of a question is that?"

The impudence! Would he be forced to justify every moment spent with Harmony?

Miss Fitzroy. Perhaps he should at least attempt to speak of her with some decorum.

Even if what he wanted to do to her was nothing close to good manners…

"A very pertinent one," returned Rogers, "when you consider you have come here to Bath under the guise of a poor musician. Do you really think people here were never going to wonder how you afforded your lodgings here in Camden Place?"

"You…mean that there is genuine interest in my person?" David felt bile rise in his throat. The last thing he wanted was for the gossipmongers to get ahold of his brother…

"Perhaps not by the entire *ton*, but certainly from a man who knows you are giving music lessons to his daughter."

David's fingers brushed up and down his piccolo, almost unconsciously, as though it was an anchor, keeping him close to shore. "He cannot think—I mean, I am only now starting to…the more time that I spend with Harmony, the more…"

Rogers coughed. "If I may be permitted to interrupt, sir, I think you are over concerning yourself. I managed to ascertain from young Seyton that the reason for the inquiries was because Mr. Fitzroy was concerned you were not being paid extra by Monsieur Bernard for the increased tuition that his daughter was receiving. His concern, believe it or not, was for your welfare."

It was then that David sat, very heavily and without much warning, onto one of the chairs in the hallway.

Thank God. He was dancing with fire here, and he knew it. Harmony Fitzroy was not a woman of no name nor family, who could be tempted into a gentleman's bed merely for the pleasure he could give her.

She was a lady. She had a family, had a father.

David took a deep breath. He needed to be careful. He wanted her, yes, but that did not mean he could have her.

"Precisely, sir," said Rogers, his tidying now complete. "I would highly recommend, sir, that you treat Miss Harmony Fitzroy well if you do find that you have an attachment to her. A father who considers those things is a man who is best to keep on your side."

And with that, Rogers strode away.

David sat, stunned, almost unable to process what he had heard. Mr. Fitzroy was clearly a better man than he had guessed.

The chimes of a quarter past the hour rang out from the open doorway into the study, and David smiled. In less than an hour, he would be with her again.

❄

DAVID'S EAGERNESS TO see Harmony again was demonstrated in three ways.

Firstly, he was wearing his second-best clothes, his coat and breeches made from dark gray satin and his favorite waistcoat, something he traditionally only kept for seeing his mother and the higher echelons of society.

Secondly, he found he was in some ways nervous, a feeling he could not recall feeling since his father received a letter from David's school saying he was failing all his subjects but music.

And thirdly, he had arrived at the Lower Rooms almost half an hour early.

It was busy today, and though David had nothing to really occupy his mind, he recognized a good many people already promenading around the room. It was all he could do to avoid their glances, but as most of them looked over and saw, not a wealthy young gentleman, but an impoverished, albeit talented musician, he was able to keep all interactions to an incline of the head.

"Goodness, Mr. Navarre, what a surprise to see you here."

David spun on his heels and broke out into a smile as he saw Miss Harmony Fitzroy casually walk toward him, an absolute dream in a pink gown with carnations embroidered across the bodice, cascading down from the skirts to the ground.

She was a vision. Remembering himself, he bowed his head.

"Miss Fitzroy, what a pleasure," he said quietly.

Looking up, David's breath caught in his throat. Each time he had thought he had seen Harmony at her most beautiful, her most captivating, she surprised him once again.

Every curl of her golden hair carefully pinned up, each link of the silver chain that lay delicately around her neck and nestled gently just above her breasts, the incredible way she smiled with her eyes before those luscious red lips, always just parted, always ready to speak; there was no one like Harmony Fitzroy.

Something stirred within David—something he knew he could not permit.

Harmony Fitzroy was not a lady for bedding. Probably.

"Let us take a turn around the room," he said in a strangled voice.

David coughed, trying to regain his composure. It would not do for him to kiss her here, in the center of all polite society—and if he did not control himself, he would do just that.

Harmony hesitated, and for a dreadful moment, David thought she was about to make an excuse—she had to return home, perhaps, and could not spend the time with him that he had been so looking forward to—but then she smiled, and took his arm.

The slight weight on his left arm was heavenly, and the clever words he usually found so easy were suddenly gone.

"How…how are you this afternoon, Miss Fitzroy," he asked.

Harmony looked up at him and smiled. "I am very well, Mr. Navarre, I thank you. I had a most pleasant day yesterday, and it has left me in a good mood."

David's face broke out in a cheeky smile. By God, she was wonderful. "Really? That is most excellent news, Miss Fitzroy. I would hate to think our music lesson was one you would not like to repeat."

"On the contrary," she said with the hint of shyness David was starting to know well, "I think I could be persuaded to make that format of music lesson a daily exercise."

David could not help it. "You tease," he whispered.

He had meant the words in jest, but Harmony looked concerned. "You think so?"

David shook his head soothingly. "It was a quip, Miss Fitzroy. I very much enjoy your wit."

Harmony returned his smile, then turned to look around the room as they walked.

David could not help but take advantage of her absent gaze to drink in every detail. *I could be with her*, he thought to himself, *and never tire.*

She seemed to be perfectly content to walk with him, just to be with him, without the need of speech. David reveled in their comfort in each other's presence—but when he saw that a small crowd of well-dressed and loud young gentlemen had just entered the room, a spark of jealously flared up within him.

Harmony's gaze drifted over to them, and David felt the red-hot spark of jealousy pierce his heart. What was wrong with him? He had never demanded a lady's sole attention before. He had never wanted to.

Harmony was different.

"I hope that your cousin, Miss Lucy, is recovered," he said, claiming her attention.

He was concerned, for a moment, that his interruption was unwelcome, but as soon as she tilted her head to face him once more, his heart soared.

"Thankfully she is almost back to full health," Harmony spoke with a smile. "I know she would be much gratified to hear you asked after her."

"It amazes me, sometimes."

"What?"

David weaved his way through a gaggle of mothers, evidently comparing notes on the Season so far. "That you have such a genuine love of your family. Most people, I think, would be astonished."

"I suppose that is true." Harmony's voice was thoughtful. "It is impossible to choose one's family, and one must accept the lot one is apportioned. I am particularly fortunate with the portion given to me."

David's hand had still not moved from hers on his arm, and he felt no compunction or desire to ever break the connection. Why should he? He wanted more. He wanted her forever.

He shook his head slightly to dislodge the thought. He was not the marrying kind, and he had to remember that. Whatever music he was making with Harmony, he had to remind himself this could go only so far.

So why was he here?

"What about you?" Her question was innocent enough. "Your family?"

David knew he should have been expecting it—but this was not a question he wished to answer in detail.

"I was fortunate, also," he said finally. "My parents greatly encouraged me in my love of music, so I was given all the support I needed to create my eleven pipers piping."

"There cannot be enough said for parents who truly believe in you, can there?"

David looked down at the woman slowly stealing away his heart and thought just how protected she had been. Her father was clearly a good man, and it gladdened his heart that Harmony had not known the familial torment and pressures that he had known.

He would not be the one to open her eyes to the vagaries of the world.

"No," he said finally.

Harmony's eyes narrowed, as though she could tell there was something amiss. All too late, David remembered her incredible ability the day before to tell when he had lied.

"None of that was true, was it?" She spoke calmly, looking at him seriously. "Your family. They didn't support your music, did they?"

David shook his head. Blast it all to hell. How did she do that? No one else was able to, not even his fool of a brother.

If he were not careful, he would find himself spilling all sorts of secrets to Harmony.

"Do they not understand what a fantastic talent you possess?" Harmony's voice was so eager, David wanted her to shout it from the rooftops. "Have they not heard you and your pipers?"

"My family has not," he said shortly.

He had been too abrupt. A look of panic flashed across the beautiful face beside him.

"I apologize," said Harmony hastily, clearly distressed. "I should not pry, David—Mr. Navarre."

A quick look around her seemed to comfort her that no one had heard the intimate tone and address she had used.

But he could not be offended. Not when she so clearly spoke from the heart. Not when that heart was encased in such a beautiful figure.

"Miss Fitzroy, I told you," David said quietly. The noise of the Pump Room thankfully covered their conversation as shouts emerged from one side of the room; politics, it appeared. "There is nothing barred from you. You can ask me anything, and I must apologize for trying to mislead you a moment ago."

She looked at him with such compassion, such brilliance in her eyes, without any judgment.

"I find discussing my family difficult," he said quietly as they reached one end of the room and turned. "I keep nothing from you that is unsavory or important, just…just a family quarrel I would rather not dwell on."

Harmony nodded and squeezed his arm.

They fell to silence again, but it was a silence shared by two who had no need to talk if they did not feel like it.

David's spirit soared. There was nowhere else he wanted to be, nowhere which could have a better claim on him than where he was right now.

Harmony chuckled slightly. It was so unlike her, so bold, that David glanced at her. "Something amuses you?"

"Only the fact," she said with a laugh, "that you do not seem to be aware almost every personage here seems to be trying to catch your eye!"

David blinked. "Now you are the one who is jesting."

"I am not," protested Harmony. "Look for yourself!"

For the first time since Harmony had entered the Lower Rooms, David looked around at the other people present and realized that she was right. So absorbed had he been with Harmony, the only beautiful person he could see in the room, that he had not noticed the curious stares he was now being subjected to by all around them.

All, that was, save for the same group of young gentlemen, who still had not taken their eyes from Harmony.

"Oh," David said as nonchalantly as he could. He had no wish to boast before Harmony, yet he wanted her to know the truth. And why not? He was proud of what he had accomplished, Tristan be damned. "That is the success of my eleven pipers piping. You must remember, I have performed in several of the great houses here in Bath, so my face is like a servants'—familiar when seen, but most people cannot put their finger on exactly why. I suppose many of them are trying to remember if I am related to their footmen."

Harmony giggled, and David smiled in turn.

"You may be correct," she said, "for look—see? Most of their gazes, given a few moments, move away from you quickly enough."

"You really do notice the strangest things, Miss Fitzroy," teased David—but then when he looked around him, he saw that she was perfectly correct.

A confused look would descend on the person looking at him, they would spend a moment or two staring, and then just like water slipping over a waterfall, their gaze would move on.

She was a marvel, moving through the world almost ig-nored—which was a travesty—yet noticing so much around her.

But Harmony was still speaking. "All of them, except that one."

David looked in the direction she indicated. "That is the Contessa Giorgia's young son, Albert."

"And why does he look at you in that way?"

He had been wondering that himself, but there was no way of telling. As far as David could remember, he had never even met him. "To be frank with you, I do not know."

"He's coming this way!" Harmony had lowered her voice to the shadow of a whisper, so David only just caught her words.

The gentleman stopped in front of them, forcing David to halt. *What did he want,* he thought bitterly, *except to talk to the most beautiful woman in the room who happened to be on my arm?*

"Mr. Navarre," said the contessa's son smartly as he bowed.

David returned the civility as quickly as he could without giving offense. "My lord."

He felt, more than saw, that Harmony curtseyed as he bowed and could not help but smile. Everything about Harmony was in time with him, as though they were being directed by the same conductor.

"I was in Manchester last week, and I happened across your brother. I was unaware you were related."

David's heart sank, but he managed to keep his composure. The last thing he wanted was for Harmony to suspect there was any cause whatsoever for him to dread the thought of contact with his brother.

Even if there was.

"I hope he was well." His curt reply did not seem to be what Albert had been expecting.

"It was a pleasure to meet him," he said almost uncertainly.

"Then I will pass on your regards," said David smoothly, "but if you do not mind, my companion and I have an appointment we simply cannot miss."

David hardly knew what he was doing; all he knew was that he had to get away from all these people. Their questions, their curiosity. He would not give them the satisfaction.

"Where are we going?" Harmony asked breathless, almost tripping in her haste to keep up with him.

"Somewhere else," he replied.

This was intolerable. Only now he looked around him did David become aware of the intensity of the Pump Room, the claustrophobic stares of others, the rumors being passed from person to person.

Society.

He had never cared much for it. Now he felt himself enclosed, unable to breathe, his strong lungs struggling to gain air.

"Ready?" David asked as they reached the door.

Harmony nodded. Without being asked, she tightened her grip on his arm and looked up at him with a smile. "Where to next?"

David thought for a moment. He could not, in all good decency, keep her with him for much longer, or there would be difficult questions for her when she returned home.

Everything in him was desperate to have her company for another few hours, at the very least, but he could not. Should not.

"I must take you home," he said sadly.

Harmony's eyes looked sad as they stepped out into the street. "Home? But David, I am…I so enjoy your company. Our meetings always seem to have the leitmotif of ending quickly."

David watched her cheeks flush slightly as she spoke, and he could not help but be pleased. Dear God, she rarely spoke her mind, he could see that, and yet she spoke to him.

Desire flickered through him, and he did not bother to repress it. Why should he? She clearly wished for another kiss. Another moment of intense pleasure.

"In that case," he said gently, turning left toward the Circus, "I will take you home—but with a slight detour."

David knew Bath so well he had already decided on the place; Queen's Park, a little-known wooded and green area that even in December, with freezing temperatures, was a pleasant place to gain some solitude.

And that was exactly what he wanted with Harmony.

"Oh, Queen's Park," exclaimed Harmony with pleasure as they rounded the corner of Gay Street.

"You know it?" David was disappointed. "I had hoped to surprise you with it."

Harmony laughed. "David, I was born here! I have lived nowhere else. You really expect to show me something new in the streets I have walked on for almost eighteen years?"

David smiled ruefully as they stepped off the street and into the quiet seclusion and splendor of Queen's Park. "I should have known better than to think I could surprise you—except," he said, suddenly pulling her into his arms and holding her close to him, "with this."

He kissed her, full on the mouth and with such a passion that he achieved his intention of surprising her.

Yet her surprise clearly did not hold her back. David groaned to feel her explore as she lifted her arms around his neck, pulling him closer. Her fingers were entwined in his hair, and his hands tightened around her as he tried to hold back, as a gentleman ought.

But Harmony Fitzroy did not make him feel like a gentleman.

David was playing the most angelic instrument ever to have graced the earth; with every movement of his fingers, smoothly running down her back to just linger for a moment on her bottom, she responded, parting her lips to give him entry.

He was gentle at first, letting her discover the new sensation—but then he could hold back no longer.

"Harmony," he said in a ragged voice. Snow was beginning to fall, and as he looked around him, he realized he was experiencing a perfect moment.

Then he tipped his head down to kiss Harmony again. He could hardly keep himself away as craving grew within him. He wanted more, and she was giving him more with each passing moment—but it wasn't enough.

This time he gradually encouraged her lips to part with his tongue, until it met her own. Her sweetness was almost too much to bear, and David could feel himself feeling…

There was nothing for it. David broke the kiss that he could have enjoyed for hours, and stared at her, eyes sharp. Her own were hazy, almost drunk with desire.

If he were bold…but no. Rushing her to his rooms and bedding her, hearing her call his name over and over again, was not appropriate. They would wonder where she was—her family.

And that was when David removed his hands from her.

"What is it?"

He could have held back. But why should he?

"I'm," said David shakily, "I'm falling in love with you."

For an instant, a horrible moment, Harmony said nothing at all. And then—

"I know," she said, her lips broadening into a smile. "Do you think I am not following you down that path?"

David blinked. It was so unexpected, so bold, and yet so perfectly in tune with the Harmony he knew, he could hardly believe it.

"I...are you sure?"

Her reply was perfect: instead of using her lips to speak, Harmony pulled down his head and gave her assent in a glorious kiss.

CHAPTER SEVEN

THE FRONT DOOR slammed, and Harmony leaned against it, heart racing.

Nothing in life had prepared her for this.

These emotions, the way she physically reacted anytime she was close to David Navarre, the indescribable kisses he rained down upon her—it was more fantastical than anything her mother had spoken of from her books!

And he was falling in love with her.

David Navarre, the most impressive musician she had ever heard, one of the few people who made her feel completely comfortable in their presence—he was falling in love with her.

Harmony had never planned to tell David how she felt about him, but that moment in Queen's Park was not one anyone could predict.

Her heart rate was slowing now, but her breath was still short. It had taken everything within her not to kiss him again when he had bid her farewell just moments ago, at the front door of her home. They had no plans to meet again, but it would be soon. It surely could not be long before she caught sight of those gray eyes again—though perhaps she would hear the lilting of his piccolo before she saw him.

Harmony sighed with a smile. Nothing could destroy this moment. Nothing at all.

"I don't understand, why have we not heard about this sooner?"

Harmony looked, startled, at the door to the drawing room. That was her mother's voice, but so unlike her. Instead of the dreamy vagueness her mother was so well known for, it was sharp and forceful and scared.

"There was no need to tell you sooner," was the reply, spoken by a voice Harmony did not recognize.

The door was closed, but the voices were so loud, she could not help but hear them. There seemed to be someone pacing in the room. What was going on?

"That's your job," her father's voice said curtly. "You are our solicitor, our advisor—that is exactly what we pay you to do. Advise!"

"Advice cannot be given before the situation is fully understood," countered the unknown voice. "As with all matters of this sort, it is best and prudent to wait for the dust to settle before any of our clients are informed."

"Yet this has lost us time!"

Harmony had never heard her father speak in such a way. Life's problems did not seem to bounce off him, as such; they never seemed to reach him at all.

When his brother, her Uncle William, and his wife, Leonora, had thought that they may lose their twin girls at birth, her father had not been concerned. It had been as though he just knew that they would survive. His compassion was for his brother and his wife and the visit that he had paid them had gone down in family history.

Turning up with a bottle of brandy to christen Isabella and Katarina, he had apparently seemed confused when Leonora was crying, telling her there was nothing at all to worry about.

He sounded worried now.

"The facts," her father demanded. "The absolute facts, give them to us now. Better late than never, Mr. Harper."

The gentleman in the drawing room with her parents

coughed, and Harmony took a silent step toward the door. She knew she should not be eavesdropping, but she could not help herself. How could she leave without knowing more?

"The facts are that you are low on financial capital. Very low, if you do not mind me saying so, madam." The man sounded a little abashed. "I would greatly advise you to make drastic changes in your lives to best protect your interests."

"Very low?" Harmony could hear her mother's voice faintly. "Just how low, exactly?"

"One thousand pounds per annum."

Harmony gasped and clapped her hands over her mouth. She stood motionless for a moment, hoping her gasp had not caught their attention, but the occupants of the drawing room had much bigger problems before them.

"One thousand pounds?" repeated her father. "You cannot be serious man, that is not enough to support my family!"

"Yet that is the situation you find yourself in."

"But the girls," said her mother quietly. It was all Harmony could do to catch her words. "Their dowries, the money we have put aside for Joy and Harmony. They are untouched, of course."

Mr. Harper's hesitation told Harmony all she needed to know.

"They are no more, I regret to say."

A crash, as if something very large—possibly her mother's sewing table—had been pushed to the floor.

"So how in God's name do you expect them to marry, Mr. Harper?"

Harmony could hear her mother sniffling and realized in horror she was crying.

She had never seen her mother cry before. Hearing it through a closed door was worse than she could have ever imagined.

"The solution is simple," Mr. Harper's voice said calmly. "You simply need to ensure your two lovely daughters do not permit addresses from gentlemen who do not have a secure enough income to support them."

"That sounded a lot simpler when they had dowries," Harmony heard her mother retort.

"Nonetheless," the gentleman continued, "it is a practicality of your situation now, not a suggestion. If they marry at all, they must marry money."

Harmony had heard enough. She wished that she had not been so foolish as to listen at all. As quietly as she could, she moved to the staircase and hurriedly went upstairs.

To think that moments ago she had been rejoicing in loving David, a musician with no support from his family, whose income from his performances surely could only be meager?

"If they marry at all, they must marry money."

Throwing herself into her bedroom, she closed the door to shut out the world.

IT TOOK SEVERAL hours before Harmony felt ready to descend, even taking her dinner in her room, but she finally regained her composure.

The idea that her parents were now at a financial disadvantage colored everywhere she looked. As she sat in the drawing room, empty now save herself, in the dark with only one candle lit, she wondered whether they could have two candles lit in the same room again.

Her gaze flickered over the sewing table, now righted, but with a scrape in the wood on one side where it had come into contact with the grate. Would they be able to replace it or mend it? Would they have to learn to live without the simplest pleasures of life?

Shuffling feet made Harmony turn, and she saw Mrs. Bird hovering in the doorway.

"Can I get you anything, Miss Harmony?" she asked softly. "You seem awfully quiet."

Harmony did not reply but stared at the woman who had

kept their home for as long as she could remember. Would they now be able to afford Mrs. Bird?

"No, I thank you," Harmony replied quietly.

Left alone, she stared out of the window. The sun had gone, and the snow which had begun when she and David had shared such intimate kisses in Queen's Park had not stopped, covering the world in a white winter blanket.

Normally, she would be delighted in the snow. But now…

"Harmony?"

Her father's voice made her look up. He appeared tired, older than she had ever seen him before.

"Hello, Father," she said quietly. "Come sit with me."

Rupert fell into the seat beside his youngest daughter on the sofa. "I have something for you here," he said quietly, holding out a small letter to her.

Harmony took it and looked at the direction. "But Father, it is addressed to you."

"I know," he said quickly, "but when I started to read the contents, I saw though it was intended for me, your eyes would appreciate a perusal."

Intrigued, Harmony could not help a bittersweet smile as she read.

Mr. Fitzroy,

I would greatly appreciate your approval for me to take your daughter Miss Harmony Fitzroy to a concert at the Assembly Rooms this evening.

If I gain your permission, I would call at eight o'clock and return her just after eleven.

The concert will be exploring the works of Bach, a composer who has not only created a great wealth of music that has torn at the souls of people around the country and abroad, but also a man I very much admire. The pieces themselves are to be played by a large ensemble including a few of my pipers, and there are parts of the phrasing I think Miss Fitzroy would gain from understanding.

I will call at eight o'clock; if I have your permission to pro-ceed, please allow your daughter to answer the door. If anyone else, I shall depart immediately and will remain your humble servant—

David Navarre

Harmony stared at every line, drinking it in, examining the way David looped the letter *l* and how his capitals were so much larger, almost unfolding onto the upper and lower lines. Even the way that he wrote was so typical of himself, grandiose and exuberant to the last.

"Thank you for showing me this, Father," she said gently, folding it back up and handing it to him. "I will ensure I do not answer the door when the bell goes."

"Not answer the door?" Rupert stared at his despondent daughter. "I would have thought you would be eager to take up this young man's offer and listen to what apparently is some of the finest music in the world. Are you not impatient to learn more for your Christmas Eve concert performance?"

Harmony nodded slowly. She could not let him see she knew. He would be mortified, and she would not force that knowledge on him.

She could bear the burden alone.

"Yes, but I am weary Papa. I do not know if I should stay out that late."

"Harmony, if it will help your music, I think that you should take this opportunity with both hands," said her father quietly. "And you can sleep all day tomorrow to make up for it."

At that very moment, there was nothing Harmony wanted to do more than sleep—but she could not avoid David forever. She would have to make a decision about him, now her parents could not permit her to consider the hand of anyone without money.

"As you wish, Papa," she said, a smile returning to her face just at the thought of seeing David again so soon. "Thank you."

The knocker on the door rapped smartly.

"I think I know who that is," said her father, rising from his seat, "and I think you should be quick to answer it before Mrs. Bird does, and she goes off into the night to enjoy Bach instead of you."

Harmony could not help but laugh as she made her way to the door—a laugh that brought a large grin to the face of the man who was standing there, waiting for her.

"It does me good to see you smile," said David Navarre, all formality gone, his greatcoat buttoned up to his neck. "Are you ready, Miss Fitzroy, for a night of delight?"

Harmony swallowed. She really should not repeat the delight she had already enjoyed with David—especially now she knew it could go nowhere, that she would have to give him up.

This could be the last time she spent with David, so she should not waste it.

"I am," she replied softly, "just wait for me to get my pelisse."

"You'll need a scarf, too!" David called after her, stamping his boots onto the ground. "'Tis bitterly cold out here, Miss Fitzroy, I do not want to dillydally!"

Harmony shook her head as she tied her father's scarf around her neck—hers was evidently borrowed by Joy and therefore could be anywhere in the house.

There was no one like David Navarre, his extraordinary music and his cavalier way with words—which is why it would be so hard to let him go. But she must. She would tell him soon.

"Come on!" urged David. "We have but twenty minutes to get there, and I have no wish for you to freeze on the journey."

As Harmony stepped out of the door, David pulled her arm into his completely naturally. The last thing Harmony saw as she pulled the front door to was her father, standing in the hallway, smiling faintly as he watched his daughter walk into the night.

Within moments Harmony saw David was right; it was bitterly cold that evening, and they hurried to the Assembly Rooms with barely two words spoken between them, focused entirely on walking rapidly toward warmth.

When they arrived, a rather pompous man was standing at the door accepting names from those who had paid for the pleasure of hearing the best music in the best setting in the best city in England.

Harmony saw David whisper into the man's ear, who nodded, and gestured for them to pass.

"I must thank you," said Harmony awkwardly. "I did not expect such a lovely surprise this evening."

"You thought I had already given you enough surprises today?" David's eyebrow arched, and Harmony could not help but laugh.

"Perhaps!"

Their laughter mingled perfectly, and Harmony's heart contracted painfully. Mere hours after declaring their growing affection for each other, she was forced to end the connection.

It was too cruel, too unfortunate.

Yet it had to be. There was no other option.

David led the way through into the room where the musicians were already seated and helped her to her seat at the end of a row, about three or four back from the front.

"Do we not want to be closer?" Harmony said in a low tone.

The atmosphere was alive with excitement, with many people seated in the audience she recognized. Her words were lost, however, in the hubbub of excited chatter and the musicians who started to tune their instruments.

David sat beside her and shook his head. "Never be closer than three rows to musicians at any time, Harmony. Yes, you will be able to hear the musician you are closest to very well, but they will drown out all the others. Here you will experience the full balance the conductor is creating for your very enjoyment."

Warmth flooded through Harmony as she tilted her head to listen. Now David had said it, she concentrated to hear each instrument, picking them out in turn—something she had not been able to do at concerts where she had dragged Joy to the front, eager to be as close to the music as possible.

"And now," whispered David, as those around them began to quiet as the conductor stood up, "we enjoy Bach."

It took just the first note to draw Harmony in. Within moments, she was caught up in the swirling melody jumping from musician to musician.

But no matter how lost she became in the music, Harmony could not ignore the presence of David Navarre seated beside her—or forget the words that she had overheard that very afternoon.

"You simply need to ensure your two lovely daughters do not permit addresses from gentlemen who do not have a secure enough income to support them."

David's music, his family's inability to support him, his threadbare coat, and his utter disinterest in money…it had seemed at the time so inconsequential.

Now Harmony knew it was imperative that she asked more. But how to begin such a conversation, both intimate and inappropriate?

Measure by measure passed, yet she could not help but want to speak.

"See the way they not only watch the conductor, but each other," whispered David, startling her from her reverie. "They move as one."

Harmony swallowed. They did indeed. But she had to speak now, she could not wait until the end of the concert. The end of the music would be the end of their time together. Forever.

"David," Harmony said nervously, "why is it that you did not wish to talk about your brother?"

"And the key part of the phrasing," David continued as if he had not heard her, keeping his voice low, "is none of them claim the title of lead, all contribute in their turn so there is perfect balance."

"When was the last time that you saw him?" Harmony persisted in a quiet voice, ignoring David's words. She had never before spoken during a concert, but she could not keep her thoughts to herself. She had to ask. "Will you be spending Christmas with him?"

"Harmony," said David, finally looking at her with a slightly hurt look. "You know that I do not wish to speak of my family."

Someone behind them coughed, and Harmony colored.

Before today she would have considered it the height of rudeness to talk during a concert, yet despite the beauty of the music surrounding them, gaining the answers to her questions was more important.

"You said I could ask you anything." Harmony tried not to let the hurt in her voice show.

"So I did," said David in a low voice, "and I said I would never lie to you, Harmony—but I can choose not to answer your question. That is my business, and it is not a pleasant one."

Harmony stared at him sadly. "How can you say that you are falling in love with me if you cannot share things with me?"

David whispered in amazement. "Harmony, I'm sharing Bach with you! I have never attended a concert with anyone I know before in my life, surely that shows something!"

She brushed aside the words, her heart contracting painfully. Music was all very well, but his life, his family—that he could not share with her?

Shame flooded her veins. She could not blame him; after all, she had not shared with him the news that this…this entanglement, whatever it was, could not continue!

"Yet basic information about your family is too much to share?" Harmony hissed.

She could not help herself. She had not hidden her own family, had introduced him to them with open arms. Yet he could not pay her the same courtesy. Tears sparkled in her eyes, but she was determined not to let him see how much this hurt her.

"I cannot help but be suspicious of you if this is not something that you are willing to impart!"

"Suspicious?" David shook his head with a sardonic smile on his face. "What could you suspect me of?"

"Where do you live, David?" Harmony returned.

She realized with a flush of heat that the musicians had increased their volume in order to rise above them.

"Camden Place," he muttered, not looking at her now, "not that my address has any bearing on this conversation."

"How can you afford to lodge in Camden Place as a musician, David?" Harmony asked, eyes wide. She hoped beyond hope he had not done something wrong, such as steal money from his family, but that was all that she could imagine right now. "How? Tell me!"

"Harmony Fitzroy!" David's temper finally flared. "You cannot egg me into revealing information I have not shared with anyone else in the world, so listen to Bach!"

But Harmony was having none of it.

"No," she said coldly. Picking up her skirts, she rose from her seat and strode as fast as she could away from David Navarre.

Not fast enough. As she stepped out onto the streets and breathed in the freezing air, a hand grabbed her arm.

"Harmony!"

"Let go," she said fiercely, wrenching her arm away as she marched down the street. Home was not far—she would be there soon.

But David did not appear to accept that. He walked alongside her, his face a picture of hurt and confusion. "I don't understand—why does this matter so much to you?"

Harmony could not put it into words. When one loved someone, a person who could not be honest, who refused to reveal basic information—how could she stand it?

Before she knew it, she was standing before her front door and pushing it open. The hallway was quiet; only then did Harmony remember that her family was visiting the Duke of Axwick.

She was alone.

"Harmony!"

Not entirely alone. David slammed the front door behind him

as he stepped into the hallway.

Harmony stepped back. "Y-You can't be in here!"

"Why not?" demanded David, fire blazing in his eyes. "If you walk away from me like that, do you not think I would follow?"

Harmony did not know what to think. As though their acquaintance had not been scandalous enough, they were now alone in her home, without her parents, sister, or cousins to act as chaperones.

She swallowed. "I…I think you should go."

David closed the gap between them and pulled her into his arms, lowering his face to almost kiss her, holding himself tantalizingly close. "Make me."

Harmony could not help it. She wanted him, wanted him in a way she had never known before, and with no one else there to stop her, she gave into temptation and lifted her lips to his own.

The gentle passion they had enjoyed by her pianoforte was not to be found here. David pushed her against the wall, his hands pinning her waist so she could not escape him.

As if she could. Harmony's eyes closed instinctively as waves of pleasure washed over her body, utterly losing herself to the myriad of sensations threatening to overwhelm her.

"Harmony…" David moaned, his chest covering hers and making Harmony feel small and delicate—and strong and powerful, all at the same time.

She clutched at him, trying to pull him closer, hardly knowing what she was doing. The kiss deepened, his tongue ravishing her own, teasing it into heights of pleasure she had never known.

Time stood still. What did it matter, now they were together?

Harmony broke the kiss and looked up at the man she knew she would love for the rest of her life. Frustration poured between them, but it was transformed into sensual desire that neither could resist.

"Come with me," she whispered.

It took them but moments to step over to her music room, David's hands never leaving her body as they did so. The instant the door closed behind them, he pulled her into his arms once more, but this time pulled off her pelisse.

Harmony's hands scrabbled at his greatcoat, swiftly dropping it to the carpet. There was not a sound outside the room; they were alone. They would not be disturbed.

"Harmony, I want..." David swallowed and took a step back, his breathing heavy.

Harmony had not noticed her own lungs struggling until now. Their ardor was making fools of them—and if they were not careful, they would soon cross a line she knew she could never undo.

His gaze pierced her own. "I want very much to make love to you, Harmony."

Her breath caught in her throat as her cheeks burned. She knew what that meant. Was she brave enough to do such a thing? To give up her innocence to a man she barely knew?

But that was nonsense. Of course, she knew him. They were musicians. They had shared something others could only dream of.

Breathing hard and wondering what on earth had got into her, Harmony did not look away from David as she slowly raised her hands to the buttons along the side of her gown.

She watched him swallow, watched his pupils dilate as her gown slowly dropped to the floor, leaving her in but her petticoats and an undershift.

"Harmony..."

David's voice was ragged, and he did not permit her to stand there alone for long. Crossing the room, he pulled her into his arms and Harmony gasped at the intensity of it. Just a few thin layers separating them, tantalizingly close...

"David!"

Harmony could not help but cry out as his hand found her breast, teasing her nipple so that shots of pleasure rocketed through her body. Her head fell back, and his mouth found her neck, that delicate spot he had first kissed, and she cried out with the joy of it all.

This was it. This was hedonistic pleasure. *Surely*, she thought wildly, *there could not be more than this?*

"Harmony, you must…" David tried to take a breath, looking down at her with his dark gray eyes. "You must be sure. I would not wish to force you, I…I need to know that you want this, too."

Harmony hesitated, only for a moment. Then her hands moved gently down to the breeches separating them and fumbled with the buttons. As she did so, her fingers grazed a long hard part of his body.

"Christ, Harmony," David moaned, his eyes closed. "I want— I need you."

To be needed, to be so desired—it was more than Harmony could ever have dreamt of.

His breeches fell to the floor and she gasped. It was…he was…

"Come here," said David quietly.

In one swift movement, he pulled his waistcoat and shirt off, leaving him entirely naked. It was madness, Harmony thought wildly. Her family could return at any moment—but then it was early…they would be at the Axwickes many hours hence.

And she wanted to know…she wanted to touch and be touched.

David led her to the pianoforte and sat himself down on the stool. "Come here."

He repeated the words, and Harmony obeyed, barely able to think as she straddled him, the skirts of her petticoats and undershift not protecting her secret place from touching—

"Oh!" Harmony barely managed to cry out at the intensity of the connection before David crushed his lips upon her own.

It was heaven. She would never again experience anything as wonderful as this. David's fingers quickly pushed her petticoats down her shoulders, freeing her breasts, which he kissed reverentially. Harmony's breathing quickened, a deep need growing inside her that she knew had to be contained—she could not let it out. She could not do what she wanted…

Then he stopped. Harmony looked down into David's eyes, her hands on his broad shoulders, that wry smile she knew so well on his face.

"Are you sure?" he whispered.

This time, Harmony did not hesitate. "Yes."

And then she moaned. David's fingers had moved to her secret place and were teasingly stroking her, her body shaking as the sharp pleasure moved through her body.

"David," she managed to gasp but that was all, her eyelashes fluttering as she rocked against his hand, needing more, not knowing what she was doing but letting her body take the lead.

It was building, building inside her, a melody so sweet that she could not believe she had never sung it before, and she was getting closer, closer to the peak until—

Harmony cried out in sweet agony.

It was several moments until she could stop her body from shaking with the pleasure of it, but as she looked at David, she saw with surprise that their lovemaking was not over.

"A little for you," he murmured with ragged breath, "and now something for the both of us. A duet."

Harmony could barely manage to breathe, but she managed to speak. "Finally, a duet between the both of us."

His strong hands moved to her bottom, lifting her up slightly. Unsure precisely what he was doing but allowing him to do so, Harmony's eyes widened as he gently lowered her onto himself.

"God, Harmony!"

His cry was music to her ears. To hear David so undone, so cracked as he attempted to restrain himself…it was wonderful. Knowing that he felt something so magnificent, too.

Harmony smiled shyly and kissed him passionately, feeling him move inside her. "I…I don't…tell me what to do."

David's gaze met hers, and Harmony knew she would remember this moment forever. Nothing could ever break the connection between them.

"R-Rise," he managed. "Then fall. Against me. Build a rhythm, as I built one for you."

Harmony obeyed—and felt a shudder of ecstasy ripple through her as she gently rose and lowered herself back onto David's manhood.

His eyes closed; his breathing quickened. A rush of power seared her heart. This was glorious, the idea of giving such pleasure. She repeated the action, and as the wave of pleasure rocked her, she saw it do the same to him.

"Oh, yes," Harmony murmured as she slowly built a rhythm of sensual decadence, pouring more and more pleasure between them. "David—"

David's jaw clenched. "I-I can't hold out much—"

"David!" Harmony cried, the same peak cresting over her once more as the symphony of their lovemaking overwhelmed her.

That appeared to be enough to push him over the edge. David poured himself into her and clutched at her as though she was the last woman in the world.

It took them several minutes to catch their breath. With David's arms around her, his face nestled between her breasts, she had no desire to move.

"That…that was…"

Harmony chuckled. "I am relieved I am not the only one to be so overwhelmed."

David raised an eyebrow as he leaned up to look up at her. "Harmony, that…"

She smiled. They had crossed the line she had promised herself she never would until she was married, but what did it matter? They would surely marry now, wouldn't they?

"And now," she said in a teasing tone, "you can tell me all about your family, and all that other nonsense you've been keeping from me."

The soft, relaxed expression on David's face disappeared. Harmony almost shrieked as he rose abruptly, reaching for his breeches.

"You think that's it?" he said in a low voice. "You think you can make love to me, and that means I must tell you everything about me?"

Harmony stared in horror. "I…well, yes!"

This could not be happening. It did not make sense—where was he going? They were engaged to be married now, weren't they? Despite her family's position, despite the pain of marriage without a dowry, they would be happy.

David did not look happy. He was staring at her as though seeing her for the first time. "Harmony, I don't understand you— you really think I cannot have secrets?"

Harmony swallowed. This was all going horribly wrong. "You still wish to keep secrets from me, a woman you've…well!"

She pulled her petticoats back up, suddenly horribly aware her breasts were exposed. It was not supposed to end like this.

David had pulled on his breeches and was now stuffing his shirt into it. "My business, Harmony, is my business, and I intend to keep it that way. Two people who love each other—"

"Should share everything," she cut across him, fire now boiling in her stomach. How had this gone so wrong? "So, I must assume you do not love me."

"Harmony you are exasperating!" David exploded, grabbing his waistcoat and attempting to put it on inside out. "Cannot you see how—"

"No, I cannot," said Harmony, tears most disobligingly appearing in the corner of her eyes. "After sharing such a—I thought we—if you cannot be honest with me, I don't want to see you again!"

"Harmony!"

This time he could not follow her. As she stumbled out into the hallway and then up the stairs, only one thought remained in Harmony's mind: that she had betrayed herself and her innocence, and all, as it turned out, for a gentleman who simply wouldn't tell her the truth.

CHAPTER EIGHT

"WHAT DO YOU think of this—perfect for your Christmas Eve concert, do not you agree?"

Harmony nodded listlessly.

For the life of her, she could not remember why she had agreed to go to Milsom Street with Joy and Esther. They had sprung it on her so early in the morning, she thought, as young ladies brushed past her desperate to find their own perfect piece of happiness in the jewelry shop they were in, that she had not had the presence of mind to decline.

She had not even found the gown she had wanted to wear, so had settled for the coral gown, which was becoming a little worn at the hem. Much like how she felt that morning.

"I knew you would like it," said Esther proudly, "and it will go perfectly with my white muslin dress, you know the one—the one with the lace added to the bottom, and around the sleeves."

Another nod from Harmony seemed to be all Esther required, and she bustled to the counter to inquire after the price of the pearl bracelet she was so taken with, her dark pelisse contrasting beautifully with her simple white gown.

"Is there anything here you like, Harmony?" Joy's voice sounded concerned, which was strange enough to hear that Harmony looked up from the ribbons she had been looking at absentmindedly.

Harmony smiled weakly. "Nothing as yet."

Partly to see how Esther was getting on with the owner of the shop, and partly to avoid Joy's stare, Harmony moved around a gossiping trio of women that had been standing behind her.

"And I heard the prince himself may be spending Christmas here, in Bath!" Harmony heard another woman say excitedly to a friend. "Can you believe it?"

Feelings of nausea rocketed through Harmony's body as she thought of the Prince Regent sitting in the audience of the Christmas Eve concert—but the conversation continued.

"Here to listen to the Eleven Pipers, that's what I heard," said the woman knowledgeably. "Navarre's pipers, you know."

"Now there's a catch," said her companion with a wicked smile. "At least, he would be if he had two coins to rub together!"

Harmony's pulse was thundering in her ears, but she had just reached Esther who looked round with a smile on her face.

"Harmony, he says it is only five shillings!"

Esther had already pulled the money from her reticule, and Harmony could see the five silver coins sitting on the counter while the man, with as broad a smile as Esther, was parceling up her treasure.

"Harmony?"

To think, she was walking around as though nothing had happened. As though she hadn't lost her innocence. As though her reputation was still perfect.

No one knew. It was strange. In an odd sort of way, she had assumed someone would be able to tell.

"Harmony!"

Harmony blinked. "My pardon, Esther, my mind was a thousand miles away. It is a beautiful bracelet, one that will perfectly reflect your splendid red hair, and I am glad you have purchased it for such a reasonable price."

"Harmony," said Joy's voice. "What is wrong?"

Harmony and Esther turned to see Joy standing behind them, a frown on her brow.

Harmony laughed nervously. "Nothing is wrong, Joy. I am…I am just a little tired from attending the concert last night, that is all."

"Here you go, miss," said the gruff voice of the shopkeeper, and Esther reached out for the little parcel bound up with a ribbon in a cutting of silk, popping it into her reticule.

"Let's go," said Joy, taking Harmony's arm rather forcefully and pulling her onto the street.

The sun was, for once, shining. It gave the world a bright and cheerful look. The snow had partly melted but there was still enough of it around to start to feel like Christmas.

Harmony could hear a lilting carol emanating from a group of singers with a bowl before them for the pennies of passersby. Holly and red ribbons adorned many of the shops along Milsom Street. The more she looked around her, the more Harmony saw that Christmas was almost here.

"Are you quite well, Harmony?" Esther spoke quietly, drawing close to her cousin. "Because I know you returned early from the concert last night, it was before the clocks struck nine. Did you feel unwell?"

"No," said Harmony, "I was just not…enjoying the concert as I had hoped. I had already told Father I was tired and did not wish to go to the concert."

Joy smiled uncertainly, a most unusual expression on her face. "I did hear Father mention you said that, that is true. Well then," she said, looking down Milsom Street at another one of their favorite boutiques. "if there is nothing wrong, let the shopping recommence!"

Esther laughed, and the three ladies continued down the street.

Harmony knew she should be enjoying this, time with her sister and cousin, yet every typical diversion tasted stale.

How could they understand: she had fallen in love with a man who clearly had no intention of being honest and vulnerable with her, and her father would never want her to marry him even if he was!

And last evening in her music room… Harmony swallowed.

It was a disaster. When she had thought about excitement and love, this was not what she had pictured.

And at Christmas, too.

Joy and Esther chattered away, and Harmony did not try to keep up with their conversation. It followed balls and gowns and whether Caroline really was going to get married the next spring or whether she was going to wait for the autumn for her parents to gain enough time to amass a suitable trousseau.

"Joy, have you—"

"I have." It was Joy's serious tone that finally brought Harmony out of her stupor. "I've seen them, and I would not concern yourself, Esther. We are in a public place, they would not dare do anything untoward, whomever they are."

"Who?" Harmony asked, looking around. "Who are you talking about, Joy?"

"Do not be alarmed," whispered Esther conspiratorially, "but we are being followed by a rather large crowd of young gentlemen—don't look, Harmony!"

Harmony whipped her head back and said quietly, "I know who they are."

"Don't be ridiculous," said Joy dismissively, "they are just young men looking for a bit of flirtatious conversation, and they are not going to get it from us."

"No, Joy, I really do know them." Harmony wrenched her arm from her elder sister's and stopped in the street. "At least…I thought I knew one of them," she said under her breath.

"Miss Fitzroy—the Misses Fitzroys, I should say," said David Navarre, smiling in the sunshine, wearing yet another greatcoat. "What good fortune to run into such young ladies as yourselves!"

"You didn't run into us, Mr. Navarre, you have been following us for a while—you and your ten pipers," Harmony said shortly. She would control herself. She would not embarrass herself nor make a scene. She wouldn't. She wouldn't do it. "And if you would be so good to leave us to our own business, I would be most grateful."

Esther was smiling, obviously intrigued. Harmony's stomach twisted painfully. She could not let her cousin strike up a conversation with any of those pipers; they would be forced to walk with them! She took her cousin's hand and continued walking.

"Come on, Esther," she said quietly.

"But Harmony," Esther protested, turning to look back at the young men. "That was Mr. Navarre, was it not? Surely he wishes to inquire whether you are quite recovered from your feelings of sickness at the concert last night?"

"Harmony's right," said Joy, speeding up as she, in turn, looked behind her, "we can gain nothing from talking to them— though they still follow us, the dogs."

Within seconds, Harmony realized there was no point in attempting to outrun David and his friends; they were all taller than they were and could easily surpass their strides.

Slowly returning to her normal walking pace, Harmony sighed. This was not what she had hoped for when she had been tempted out of doors with promises of fripperies and jewels.

"Miss Fitzroy, you and I have business to discuss!" David called after her. "And I am sure your sister and cousin would like to be introduced to some of my good friends here."

"Some of them are remarkably handsome, you know," said Esther with pink in her cheeks. "Would it be so dreadful to stop and talk to them?"

"Yes," said Harmony briskly. "The last thing I want to do at this very moment is talk to Mr. David Navarre!"

But that was not to be.

"Good morning, ladies," said David, jogging around them by stepping into the road so quickly that a carriage had to swerve to avoid him. "May I be so good as to borrow Harmony for a moment?"

"Borrow her?" Joy had been forced to come to a halt and she

was not pleased about it. "My sister is not some book you can borrow from a lending library, Mr. Navarre!"

"I spoke in haste," said David gently, arms open to show he meant no harm. "I just want to ascertain how she is feeling."

"I am quite well, thank you, Mr. Navarre," said Harmony. She wanted desperately to gaze into his gray eyes but avoided looking at him directly at all costs. "And I would like to be on my way now."

"Let me introduce you to some of my pipers," David said smoothly, encouraging his friends to join him. There were now gentlemen all around them, and Harmony could not help but feel intimidated. To be sure, none of them looked ungentlemanly, but having all exits from David's presence cut off completely felt like a trap.

"Gentlemen, this is Miss Joy Fitzroy, her sister Miss Harmony Fitzroy, and their cousin Miss Esther Fitzroy."

Heads bowed around them, but without even raising her head, Harmony could tell David had not looked away from her for one moment.

What did he want with her?

"Pleased to meet you, gentlemen," Esther curtseyed but was the only one of the three of them to do so.

Finally, Harmony could prevent herself no longer. She tilted her gaze slightly and saw David looking at her intently, a smile playing about his lips but a nervous one at that.

He was not so sure of himself, Harmony thought. It was so unlike him that the knot in her stomach loosened slightly.

"Miss Fitzroy," he said quietly as his pipers went round introducing themselves, "how are you feeling?"

"Well, thank you." Harmony spoke stiffly, anger growing that he had put her in this position. "None of us have caught Lucy's cold yet."

"You know what I mean," said David, taking a step forward toward her. "I don't want to know about your health. How are you feeling?"

Harmony swallowed but used the continuing chatter around her to speak so Joy and Esther would not be able to hear her. "Torn. Conflicted. Whatever it is that you do to me, David Navarre, it is confusing, and I do not like it."

David hesitated for a moment, as if deciding on something, and then nodded to himself. Reaching forward, he grabbed her wrist and started to pull her with him as he strode down the street.

"David!" Harmony cried, quite forgetting that in public he should always be Mr. Navarre. She glanced back at her sister and cousin—why had they not noticed she had been pulled away from them? "What are you doing—where are you taking me?"

"Not far," he said, "and if you are quiet this will not take long."

Panic flared up in Harmony's heart. Surely David would not do anything to harm her, would not do anything untoward?

But then, the David that she thought she knew would surely have nothing to hide, nothing to hold him back. But what did she really know of his character?

He had not told her the truth…

"Harmony," he said quietly, turning the corner onto Burton Street, a much quieter and smaller road, without so many eyes watching, and pulled her down into a small alleyway. They were alone. He let go of her hand and raised his own to her face. "Harmony…"

He leaned in to kiss her, the very thing she had been longing for him to do ever since she had noticed him following her with his pipers, but it could not be—she would not permit him to.

Harmony pushed him away.

"Don't," she said quietly. "Now what is it you want? How could you separate me from my family?"

"It is only for a moment," replied David, his face serious, "because what I want to say cannot be said in front of them. It is for your ears only."

Harmony shook her head, heart racing. This was all wrong—

if she were found here… "I don't want to hear it."

"You don't even know what I am to say," protested David, "and you were the one who stormed off last night after we made love!"

Harmony glanced at the slither of street she could see at the alleyway mouth. No one seemed to be about.

As Harmony paused to gather her thoughts, she thought once more of the conversation that she had overheard.

"Now there's a catch. At least, he would be if he had two coins to rub together!"

"David," she said quietly. "You know how I feel about you—"

"And I, you," David urged quietly, taking a small step toward her. There was no way to escape him—even if she had wanted to. "Which is why I do not comprehend why you abandoned me last night."

"David, where is this going?" Harmony said with bewilderment, her voice lowering to a whisper. "This is not how courtships are done! This is not how people meet! What we have shared is accidental meeting, chaos, musical concerts, confusion, and emotions so strong," and here her voice caught in her throat, "so strong I have not known what to do with myself!"

"Just because we are not like everyone else, does not mean that being together is wrong!" David smiled faintly. "We are different, you and I. It is as though we were brought together by fate or chance or music!"

Harmony laughed as she shook her head. "Where…where is this going?"

She hardly knew what she wanted his answer to be.

"I want to marry you," said David shortly, "and I don't know when or how or what our marriage will look like—I hope it will be full of music and love and laughter."

His words struck right into Harmony's heart and soul. She could picture them together, sharing a music room, writing music together, spending their days in a happy haze of orchestras and concert halls.

But then her father's face loomed in her imagination, and she looked at the ground bitterly. "I cannot marry you."

It took a moment for those words to sink in.

Then David said, "Why would you say that, Harmony? After all we've shared, after we…I don't…do you not love me?"

"You know I do," said Harmony desperately, ignoring his overtures, "but I know you, David! I know what you are."

Memories whirled around her head: the question her father had put to him when he had come to her home; his own admission that musicians were paid poorly. Monsieur Bernard's lodgings that had not changed in décor or contents since her earliest memories—and then her father's solicitor, Mr. Harper's, words when describing her inability to marry without money: *"it is a practicality of your situation now, not a suggestion."*

He was an impoverished musician, entirely unsuitable for her family now. It did not matter what she felt, what they felt for each other.

That was the truth of it.

DAVID STARED AT her, aghast.

How could she have found out? How could she know? The fact he had abandoned his family to play his music was the secret he had tried his hardest to keep from almost everyone. The truth—that he was a wealthy man independently—had also been hidden, because he had not wished for the fawning irritation of ladies.

Yet that did not matter to Harmony Fitzroy.

Wealth? She did not care for it, evidently. Only now did David realize how painful it was, to be so rejected. She knew the truth of it, though God knew how, and yet she still did not want him.

He stared at the sadness in her eyes and saw that being a musician with no regular pay, no financial income to speak of save for an inherited fortune—and more importantly, a man who had left his family and friends to pursue his dream, with no thought for the consequences—was not something any man would be proud of. Any father would be.

Any wife.

"I know what you are," Harmony repeated, tears in her eyes, "and that is just not enough for my family."

Her words cut into him like daggers.

Of course, it's not, he thought bitterly. Look at the way Mr. Fitzroy protected his family and cared for anyone that came into contact with them. That was her model of a husband, of a father. *I don't come anywhere close. For all she knows, I could just leave her as easily as I left my own family.*

Harmony's cheeks were wet. For a second, he thought she was crying, his heart tearing into pieces—but a quick glance up at the sky told him it had started snowing again.

David swallowed. He could not speak, could not move. So thrown by Harmony's words, he felt as if she had run him through with a blade.

How could he blame her for such a reaction? She was being true to herself, true to what she wanted.

What she deserved.

And Harmony Fitzroy did deserve the best. How could he condemn her for that?

"So, you would forsake me for your family," David said finally, unable to keep the bitterness from his voice, "because I am not good enough for them."

"I would choose you if I knew you would choose me," Harmony said softly, "but you...you do not trust me, David. You have not shared things with me, and now no matter what I have heard, no matter what different decision I may have made if I did not know the things that I do now, we must part."

Who could have told her—but the truth was, it did not really matter. Nothing really mattered now, beyond the woman that was standing before him. What mattered was that it should have been him to tell her, and now that she had learned it another way, Harmony Fitzroy was lost to him.

"I see," David said curtly, trying not to let his hurt show. "Well, I shall leave you then—and I wish to God I had not fallen in love with you. I do not think you require any more music lessons from me, so you will not be burdened with my presence again. Good day, Miss Fitzroy."

And with that, he turned on his heels and stalked away, attempting to ignore the tears falling down his face, mingling with the falling snow.

CHAPTER NINE

CHRISTMAS EVE WAS meant to be one of the happiest days of the year. In the Fitzroy household, the complete opposite was currently true.

The entire household was reeling from Harmony's sadness, which had continued for over a week now.

"It's Christmas Eve," whispered Lucy, looking nervously at Harmony, seated on the other side of the room. Harmony attempted not to show she could hear her cousin. "I would have thought that she would have recovered by now."

"How can we know that?" Joy said irritably, seated at the table with her portable writing desk, paper and pen before her but nothing written. "We do not even know for sure exactly what it is that has upset her!"

Esther shook her head as her embroidery sat in her lap, untouched. "We do not know the details, that is to be sure, but we certainly have a good idea as to the nature of the cause."

The three young women were sitting in the drawing room, attempting to distract themselves. Harmony sat in the window seat, gazing out onto the snow-filled street. She had not spoken for most of the morning. She had no wish to.

That did not prevent her cousins and sister from speculating.

"I heard muffled crying from her room yesterday," whispered Lucy.

Harmony flushed but did not look round. She would not give them any further cause to talk about her. Surely if she just sat here quietly, they would eventually think of another topic?

"Well," said Esther darkly, "I can think of but one cause for that."

Harmony bit her lip and tried her hardest not to look around.

Despite the fact that Mrs. Bird had decorated the whole house for Christmas, holly and ivy adorning each doorframe, candles throughout the home in beautiful colors and scents, and a sprig of mistletoe hanging by the front door, there was no festive feeling in the Fitzroy home.

"Men!" Joy sniffed. "You know, the hurt of my little sister has pained me far more than I could ever have imagined. I have no idea what Mr. Navarre said to her that day in Milsom Street, but I wish his words had never been uttered!"

Lucy had a book opened but unread in her hands. "I had no idea Harmony knew Mr. Navarre that well, let alone had…well. An understanding with him."

Harmony's cheeks burned. If only they knew. If only they had the slightest idea what she and David had—but perhaps it was better if they did not know. The last thing she needed was scandal, or for her father to feel as though she had been ruined forever.

Though perhaps that would not matter. After all, it was not as though she or Joy would ever be married, not without dowries.

Joy shrugged. "Who is to say they did? At the very least, Harmony had an inclination for him, and he must have known that—why else would he have followed us so determinedly, and pulled her away from us to speak with her?"

"We cannot know that, for sure," said Esther, a helpless look on her face, her embroidery stark against her white gown. "I mean, surely Harmony would have told us?"

"You know Harmony," Joy said, shaking her head. Harmony could feel their gazes on the back of her neck. They could at least whisper, pretend that they were speaking about something else. "She has always been shy, it has always been such a struggle to get anything out of her, even the small things. If she really did have affection for Mr. Navarre, then—"

Harmony turned her head to see Esther who was suddenly engrossed completely in her embroidery. Joy was apparently writing a letter furiously. Lucy's entire face was hidden by a book—a fact Harmony would not normally have noticed had the book not been upside down.

"How are you getting on," asked Harmony. She would have laughed if pain had not been so embedded in her soul.

Her sister and two cousins murmured but none raised their eyes to meet hers.

"When will you practice your pieces?" asked Joy quietly, not looking up from her letter. "For the Christmas Eve ball?"

Harmony swallowed. It was not a topic anyone had broached with her in days, but they could not help but have noticed.

She had not touched her pianoforte since she had last spoken to David.

Well, how could she? After they had…after everything they had shared there. The music, the kisses, the lovemaking…

"I just do not want to practice, right now," she said quietly.

After several minutes of silence, Esther finally put down her embroidery, looked at Harmony, and smiled. "Harmony, do you want to help me with this delicate piece here, in the left corner?"

Harmony shook her head, concentrating on her fingers in her lap. "I do not wish to do anything."

Her eyes flickered around the room. She had refused to join in with decorating the home, much to the surprise of her family. It had been the first time she had not, and although her mother had even roused herself from her book long enough to exhort Harmony to join in, she could not.

Everywhere she looked, she saw not gaiety and joy, but expense. How much had those scented candles cost? How long would they last? They had not managed to get enough holly from their garden this year, so how much had her father had to spend on the extra sprigs required?

Everywhere she looked was another reminder that her parents were going to have to spend Christmas very differently hereafter.

"You must want to do something," said Joy, her voice softer than usual. "Even if it is something small. I have not heard you play the pianoforte in above a week now."

"I have no wish to play it," was the sullen reply Harmony gave.

How could she explain it to them—that whenever she had tried to sit at her pianoforte, she was tortured by the memories of David, his strong arms playing the pianoforte as she had never played before, the gentle kiss on the side of her neck which started everything—

No. She could not think that way, she could not go down that path.

She had been willing to go down the aisle with him, yet he could not even tell her why he did not see his family? That was not love. What was love without trust?

Lucy lowered her book. "That is so unlike you, Harmony. Whenever you have been upset before, your one solace has been your pianoforte."

Harmony sniffed bitterly. The fact her cure and her sickness were the same had not gone unnoticed.

"How about a Christmas carol?" Esther said brightly. "You could play it, and we will all come through and sing it!"

"What about *Hark the Herald*?" Lucy seemed eager enough to join in but looked nervously at Harmony as she spoke. "Or *While Shepherds Watched Their Flocks by Night*?"

Despite their efforts Harmony was just as despondent as when she had first returned home from the unfortunate shopping trip in Milsom Street. She still avoided their gazes, and the more that they tried to lift her spirits, the more they sank.

They couldn't know…they hopefully would never know the

agony of sharing oneself with a gentleman, and then…then knowing he could not love you in the way you wanted. The way you needed.

"I am not going to play," Harmony said evenly in a low voice. "I have already sent my note of regret to Monsieur Bernard to communicate that I will not be performing at the Christmas Eve concert tonight. Let that be an end to it."

"Not play in the Christmas Eve concert?" Esther gasped. "Harmony, you have been talking about it for weeks, it was the highest honor that you as a musician have ever been paid! I thought that you would be leaving in the next few hours to get there!"

"I have already chosen my outfit," said Lucy in a confused voice. "I do not understand, you were so looking forward to playing tonight!"

"Just leave me be," Harmony said quietly. "I have no wish to entertain or be entertained, I thank you."

If she had hoped these words would have encouraged them to leave her alone, Harmony was very much mistaken.

In a swirl of skirts, Joy turned round from her desk, her eyes flaring in the way that her family had learned to avoid. Harmony winced, expecting the incoming storm.

But it did not come.

"Harmony, we love you," said Joy softly. "We want you to be happy. You do not have to tell us what has occurred between you and…anyone else. But if we can make you happy, in any way, please tell us. I would do anything for you, you know that."

Tears sprang to Harmony's eyes, and she immediately rose. She would not cry in front of her family—crying in front of David had been bad enough.

"Harmony, wait—"

But no words could keep Harmony in the room. She ran straight into her father.

"My word, Harmony!" he said. "I did not realize the summons to war had been declared! Where are you going in this swift manner—ah, I had forgotten the Christmas Eve concert. Make sure that you save enough seats for us, we will all be joining you."

Harmony colored. Blast. She had not told him. "My apologies, Father, I did not mean to jostle you so. I…I am not playing at the Christmas Eve concert tonight so there will be no need for any of you to stir from the house on this cold night."

Rupert blinked in confusion. "Not…not play?"

Shaking her head, Harmony continued, "So I am just going to return to my room, Father, there will be no need to send anything or anyone up to me."

She had almost passed her father on the way to the stairs when he reached out and gently placed a hand on her shoulder.

"Come with me."

There was nothing for it. She did so meekly, until both of them were standing in the music room. The cover had been placed over the pianoforte by Harmony the day she had returned from her altercation with David, and it had already started to gather a little dust.

Her heart twisted to see it. When had she last left her pianoforte so long it had gathered dust? She could recall no such instance.

She did not wish to be scolded by her father, and so she drew herself up, as ready as she could be for his words.

Rupert faced his youngest daughter. "You know, Harmony, it is only now I look at you properly that I realize you have been much downcast these last few days. Those heavy eyes full of sadness, the way your mouth has not smiled in over a week, and more importantly, the total lack of music in this house, is starting to concern me."

Harmony shook her head wearily and tripped out the same excuse. "Do not worry, I simply feel unable to—"

"No, that's not it," interrupted her father. "Now I know you, better than even you do, and when I say there is something seriously wrong here, that is exactly what I mean. Now then," and he stepped forward, positioning the pianoforte seat opposite the one David had sat on, "sit down and tell me all about it."

Rather unwillingly, Harmony sat on the pianoforte seat, and her father sat opposite her. It was strange for her to sit in this seat without the keys before her, and her fingers tingled as they felt they should be creating music by now.

Rupert watched his daughter closely. "I have all night, you know."

"I know," Harmony smiled weakly. "And I have always trusted you, Father, to know what is best for me. I know circumstances have changed, and in a way, I can respect your change of decision. But," and her voice cracked under the pressure of preventing tears, "it is so very hard, now I have met a gentleman I so greatly admire, to remove him from my life so entirely—it is painful."

"Harmony," said Rupert slowly, "I am confused by so many aspects of your speech, I hardly know where to begin!"

"But in a way," continued Harmony, her gaze flickering over to the pianoforte unconsciously, "it is a good thing. I mean, he could barely share the most basic of information with me. It does not really matter if I love him, does it Father, if he cannot do that?"

Rupert shook his head. "Love? Gentleman? Remove from your life? Harmony, I have evidently been remiss in my care of you if so much has occurred this Christmas I have been so woefully unaware of!"

"It does not matter now," said Harmony gently. She could not speak of it in detail, in any event. Even these short words had been painful. "You see, I know I can no longer marry for love, and although it pains me, I see the necessity."

"Harmony Fitzroy," her father said sternly, "if you do not start to make some sense, then I am going to make you re-enter this room and start the conversation all over again!"

She swallowed. She had not thought of revealing the source of her knowledge, but now she appeared to have no choice.

Her cheeks burned as she spoke. "I...I heard. And I am sorry,

Father, I have never done so before, but I had just returned home and so could not help overhearing your conversation with Mr. Harper!"

Vague understanding started to dawn on Rupert's face. "Ah…Mr. Harper. You heard that our finances are somewhat diminished from what we had thought?"

Harmony nodded, silent.

"And then," he continued slowly, "you would have heard that the money that we had put aside for your dowry, and that of Joy's, had also gone."

A single tear dropped from Harmony's eyes, but she dashed it away quickly. "I do not blame you, Father, you must know that. I want to be helpful in any way that I can."

"But there is still something that I do not understand," said her father. "Tell me exactly what you heard."

Harmony swallowed at the painful memories, then spoke quietly. "I heard Mr. Harper saying we—Joy and I—would need to ensure we married wealthy men. That we would not be able to marry for love alone, that monetary matters would need to be certain first."

"And then?"

"And then," said Harmony with a sniff. "I went upstairs. I had come home with such euphoria in my heart, but hearing that…well, that we would be unable to choose our husbands with our hearts quite took all the elation from me. I went upstairs to my room."

Her father shook his head. "So, you have been thinking since that dreadful man came here with his nonsense that you are now barred from marrying?"

"Not marrying," Harmony interjected. "Just…marrying for love."

There was a rather strained and awkward silence between them after this pronouncement. Harmony could hardly bear to look at her father. She had meant what she said—she did not blame him.

But it was hard to give up a man like David Navarre.

"Darling child, you take too much of the worries of this family on yourself!" her father said gently. "Did you think I would let that ridiculous man Harper talk such nonsense in my home and about my two precious daughters?"

Harmony stared. The idea the conversation in the drawing room she had been overhearing had continued after she had gone had not even occurred to her.

"My precious Harmony, I would lay down my life if it meant you could marry for love," her father said gently, reaching out his hands to enclose hers. "Your happiness cannot be counted in shillings and guineas, and I would never want it to be."

Another few tears fell from Harmony's eyes as she whispered, "Really?"

"Definitely." He gave her a concerned smile. "And that is along the lines of exactly what I said to the imbecile Harper before he left. Now, what has this done?"

Harmony smiled wanly at him. "What do you mean?"

"You speak of a gentleman," said her father, "a gentleman you clearly have a great deal of affection for—but it seems as though his pockets are not as full as they could be. Is this why you have…what did you say? 'Removed him from your life entirely'?"

Harmony nodded wretchedly. "But Papa, he made it so difficult for me! I will admit," and here some of the old Harmony resurfaced as she smiled at him, "I was considering going against what I had thought were your wishes to be with him!"

"You love him," he said softly.

Harmony found that she could not speak, so she nodded instead.

"Yet despite your love for him, and I would imagine his love for you, despite your decision to go against what you thought was my will, you have broken with him?"

Harmony nodded once more. "Father, he is so frustrating! There is so much about his family, about himself I do not know, and he will not tell me!"

Rupert released his daughter's hands as he leaned back and laughed. "Oh, Harmony, do you really think that a man and a woman know absolutely everything about each other when they marry?"

Unsure of herself and a little piqued that her father could laugh about such a serious situation, Harmony said, "But Father, it was inconsequential information!"

"Inconsequential for you, perhaps," he returned. "You have the blessing of a loving home and, I hope, two parents who adore you and care for you the best way that they can. But you know, that is not the sort of home that your mother had."

Harmony stared. She had never heard her mother speak of her family before—she had been an orphan when her parents met. Or at least, that was what she had been told. "Mama?"

Her father shook his head sadly. "I had to learn there were certain questions your mother did not want to answer when we first married. The hurt that had been done there was such a fresh wound, and she did not want to open it up again."

"And now?"

He sighed. "There are elements of her past I still do not know, I am sorry to say—but much has been shared with me as we have grown together in love and kindness. You see, Harmony, marriage is not the end of the journey. It is merely a turn in the road, giving you a new perspective, a new view. You may not be able to see all of the path your partner took to get to you, but that is not the important thing."

"What is?" Harmony whispered, her heart fluttering.

"That they got there, and they met you, and they chose to forge a new path with you in married life," said her father simply. "That is all that really matters."

Harmony sat there, stunned.

She looked back at her time with David; each meeting he had shared himself with her in a way he had done with no one else before. She had watched him practice when he had thought he was completely alone—and then had not been embarrassed or angry with her, but had welcomed her and included her in a concert. He had spoken about his music and played with her and walked with her and laughed with her and the whole time, he had asked nothing of her.

And when he had taken her in his arms…it was a moment she never thought she would experience. A joining of two hearts, two minds, two souls, two bodies that desperately wanted each other.

Some time had passed before she spoke again.

"I love him," Harmony said with a shy smile.

"And I give you my blessing," said her father beaming, "if young Mr. Navarre is the man of your choice. Because I would never prevent you from marrying for love. As long as there is love and a desire to walk the path together, that is enough for me."

Harmony sprung from her seat with only one thought in her mind. "I have to go to him!"

"I know," he said mildly. "Just make sure that you wrap up warm. Mrs. Bird has told me the snow is coming down rather heavily."

Kissing her father on the cheek, Harmony rushed out into the hallway, grabbing a pelisse with one hand and a large scarf with the other. She had opened the front door before she had managed to get either of them on, and as she ran along the road, she struggled to tie the fastening on her pelisse.

Her father and Mrs. Bird had been right, the snow was certainly coming down hard, and it would be a very white Christmas tomorrow—but it would not be a happy one, Harmony thought wildly, if she could not get to the Christmas Eve concert in time!

She had no idea what the hour was, but she was determined to get to the Assembly Rooms as soon as possible.

As Harmony ran, breath catching and pouring out of her in white puffs, her heart was pounding so hard she could barely hear anything else.

There was the Assembly Rooms, and there were still plenty of people milling around. Her spirits soared—she was not too late!

Ignoring the protestations of the footman standing at the doorway, Harmony pushed past countless people ignoring their cries as she knocked a few older gentlemen into each other.

Her only thought was to get to David before the concert began.

And then she was there. Heart still beating rapidly, her eyes darted around the room to see if they could lock onto a pair of gray eyes.

But then her brow furrowed. The people milling around were not moving toward their seats, they were moving away from them. The musicians were fiddling around with their instruments, but putting them away, rather than tuning up.

Understanding dawned in Harmony's mind, and it was painful.

She had missed it. She had missed her chance to speak to David. He was gone.

Harmony pulled off the scarf wildly wrapped around her neck, and let it fall to the floor, bitterly disappointed. This, she thought dully, was it then. She had missed her chance at happiness. The Christmas Eve concert came but once a year, and she had let Monsieur Bernard down this year. He would not invite her for a second.

But far more importantly, she had lost the chance to be with the only man she knew she would ever love.

The gentleman who completed her, whose tune of life perfectly matched hers. David Navarre.

"Harmony?"

CHAPTER TEN

HARMONY KNEW THAT voice, she would know it anywhere. Every lilt and tone was beloved.

"David?"

She turned to see a tall man dressed in black and white, holding a piccolo in one hand and music in the other, his gray eyes trained on hers as if he was looking at an apparition.

"Harmony," David said weakly, "what are you doing here?"

There was no conscious thought in what Harmony did, she only did what she knew she had wanted to do for days now, and with David just standing there, she took her chance. Rushing toward him, she threw her arms around his waist and hugged him as if he was the last anchor in a storm.

"David," she murmured, glorying in the tower of strength he was, breathing in his comforting scent.

There was a crash, and Harmony felt David's arms enclose her in a crushing embrace. The treasured piccolo had fallen to the floor in his eagerness to hold her again.

Harmony pulled away from him to look into his face, and though there was a smile there, it was serious.

"You didn't come," he said, confusion and sadness mixed in his expression. "To the concert. Why did you not perform with me?"

Harmony had only one answer to that, and it was one she

gave willingly—a crushing kiss, giving herself completely over to the freedom of it all. David responded eagerly, and with no thought to the countless people around them, they clung to each other, the kiss deepening with every heartbeat.

The kiss ended but Harmony kept her face close to David's, noses touching. "I'm so sorry," she said, emotion almost overwhelming her voice. "I am sorry I did not come."

"I could not believe your hatred of me was strong enough to keep you away from performing," said David, sadly. "To think that my actions took away your chance of performing in the Christmas Eve concert here—I shall never forgive myself."

Harmony could hear the gasps and the gossip that was at that very moment erupting around them, but what did she care for them? She was in David Navarre's arms, and she was never going to let him go again.

"I've been so foolish," she said with a splutter of laughter, "and everything I did was under false information to start with, so it matters even less!"

"I just don't understand," said David quietly. "One moment we had told each other we loved one another, and we shared…and the next, you have broken with me! Of course, once you found out my secret, the way I had worked to keep the truth away from people—"

"Secret?" Harmony stared, confused. "What secret?"

Secret? Harmony's heart fluttered painfully at the word. So, there was a secret he had not been telling her, then? Or was it something entirely different?

"Harmony, you said so yourself in the alleyway when I tried so desperately to keep you from breaking off…whatever it was we were."

Harmony laughed. "David, I have absolutely no idea what you are speaking of!"

A cough behind her made Harmony, albeit reluctantly, turn her head away from David. A man was standing there, looking most disapproving.

"Excuse me," he said gravely, looking past Harmony to David, "but I believe, sir, that this conversation could be had in a more appropriate location."

"Damnit, Rogers," burst David, "your timing has never been so at fault!"

Harmony twisted her head between the man she loved and the man who seemed intent on interrupting them—yet David seemed to know him?

"Nevertheless, I can provide you with an area which may be a little more private," said the man quietly, inclining his head toward a door to their right.

David sighed and finally let go of Harmony. He leaned down to pick up his piccolo and with his other hand, took Harmony's.

"Come on," he said in a low voice, "we'd better do what Rogers says, or I shall have to endure it later."

Harmony walked with David to the door, and it was only after they had both gone through it and he had shut the door firmly that she asked, "Who was that?"

"Rogers? Oh, he's my butler. He does everything for me really." David treated her to one of his cheeky smiles. "Why, have you decided to throw me over for him? He does a very good steak and kidney pie, I will admit, but he can't play the piccolo to save his skin."

"No," giggled Harmony, poking David in the chest, then drawing closer to him. "I didn't know that you had a butler."

"There is a lot that you do not know about me," said David, a serious tone creeping back into his voice again. "And that is my fault. I can understand why you did not wish to marry me. I should never hold things back."

Harmony kissed him on the cheek, then found her ardor was too much to resist kissing his mouth again. He responded heatedly, pulling her close to him, and the kiss deepened until they were forced to draw breath.

"I was wrong to push you away," she said softly, "though I had no idea why you needed to hold back such things. What good did it do me, trying to force it from you?"

"But you should know," said David. He pushed her away, though with regret in his eyes, and Harmony wondered whether he, too, was having to fight the need to continue kissing as though their lives depended on it.

It was only then that Harmony started to look around the room they found themselves in. It seemed to be a storage room.

David sat down on a chair. "You see, Harmony," he said awkwardly, "music was not the sort of thing my parents wanted me to invest my time in. They were passionate about the family business, and they wanted both myself and my younger brother—younger by but one year—to commit our whole lives to it."

Harmony could tell that this was difficult for David to say, so she stood still and quiet, letting him speak at his own pace.

"My brother and I...we have never got on, and we are very different people." David's face was sad. "I believe if we met now as general acquaintances, neither of us would wish to befriend the other. As it was..."

David's voice trailed off, and Harmony gazed at him with love. No wonder David had struggled to impart even the smallest detail to her about his family. No wonder he had been so impressed and envious at her closeness with her sister and cousins.

She could not imagine being so distant with a family member. Why, to all intents and purposes, David was alone in the world.

"Please," she said quietly, "you do not have to tell me all of this if you do not want to."

But David was shaking his head. "Harmony, I want you to become my whole life, the person I live my life with. Not sharing such things with you was wrong, and though I cannot possibly fathom how you found out that I had abandoned my family and the family business to come here—"

"But I didn't," said Harmony, finally realizing from where the confusion had come. Oh, it was all so stupid, so easily remedied. If only she had thought to explain herself fully. "When I spoke that day about learning something that would keep us apart, it was something about my own family that I was referring to, not yours."

"Yours?" David sounded perplexed. "Harmony, your family is the height of respectability!"

"At the moment we are," she said sadly. "But…you remember that day we returned from the Lower Rooms, with the slight," and here Harmony smiled at him wickedly, "detour into the Queen's Park?"

"Remember?" David shook his head with a smile. "You cannot imagine how that day is ingrained in my memory!"

Harmony smiled, the memories pervading her mind. "That day, when I returned home, I overheard a discussion between my parents and their solicitor."

David sat up sharply. "A discussion?"

"An argument really." Harmony knew her father would not mind this intimate piece of family knowledge being shared with David. After all, was he not about to become a part of the family? "Much of their fortune has been lost, and I heard Mr. Harper—their solicitor and advisor—tell my parents that Joy and I would no longer be permitted to marry for love. That we would need to marry for money, or at least ensure there was enough money if there was a vague amount of affection."

David's mouth had fallen open. "Harmony, I had no idea! I wish you had told me, but…this may be presumptive of me, but…well, I would not have thought that your father would have agreed with that."

Harmony laughed as she shook her head. "How is it that you have clearer insight into him than I do? Yes, you are correct. My father stated he would never restrict Joy and me for marrying for love."

"Then," said David helplessly, "I don't understand."

"I did not hear his reply," said Harmony simply, shrugging her shoulders. "I had become so overwhelmed I might not be able to…that we could not…I left and heard no more, and I have only now, this very evening, heard the full extent of the conversation."

"To marry without love is abhorrent to me," said David quietly.

"And to me," said Harmony, "but what upset me most was that I realized that I was so in love with you that I was perfectly willing to go against Mr. Harper and my parents and anyone in the world if it meant that I could be with you—but you did not seem willing to even speak to me on certain subjects. I see now that that was wrong," she said as David tried to protest, "and my father has given me his blessing. That is," she said hastily, "if you still…want to marry me."

For a moment, Harmony thought he did not. He sat motionless, without speaking, his gray eyes cast down as though unwilling to look at her.

Her breath caught in her throat. She had missed her chance, then. It was all over.

David rose and swept Harmony into his arms. He rained down kisses onto her just like the snow falling outside, until he found her lips and ravished them, so great was his passion.

"Harmony, I want to marry you very much," David said jaggedly when he had the presence of mind to speak, "but I still do not understand why, even if your father had agreed with Mr. Harper, that would have prevented us from being together?"

Harmony blinked up at him, eyes clouded with desire. "Well," she said awkwardly, "I know musicians have very low incomes. You are not rich, David, you are poor, and I thought—"

"What on earth," said David slowly, "has given you the impression that I am not rich?"

Harmony laughed softly. "Come now, David, do not jest, I am in earnest."

"And so am I," David said, raising a hand to cup her face. "Harmony, my love, the secret I have brought with me here to Bath, all the way from Manchester, the secret I have tried to keep all here from knowing, the secret that I had thought you had finally discovered, is that I am…well, let us say that I am quite the opposite of poor."

Harmony understood the words, but they surely could not have the meaning that she thought. "The opposite of poor?"

The room was spinning and only partially due to the tingling memory of pressure on her lips.

David laughed. "Harmony, if it were not so vulgar, I would confidently say I am fabulously rich! The family business in Manchester? I inherited absolutely all the capital."

Unable to say anything, Harmony just looked at him and stared. Rich. David, rich? It did not make sense. He was one of the worst attired people she had ever seen.

And yet…yet was it not the very wealthy who were able to do such things? Play music to his heart's content, without worrying about an income? Wander around in last year's fashions with threads at the end of sleeves merely because one could?

Was it not he who had secured their invitation to the contessa's?

He was wealthy. They could marry and marry for love. Harmony could hardly believe it.

"Harmony," said David gently, "it means more to me than I can say that you would part with your family and your father's good opinion to be with me and marry me, even though you believed I was not wealthy. I admit, I am in some ways sad to inform you that if you do decide to marry me, we shall have to curtail our spending to fall into my yearly income of twelve thousand pounds."

Harmony stared at him. "Twelve—twelve thousand pounds!"

It was a ridiculous sum. A sum worthy of a duke. Twelve thousand pounds?

"Does this mean that you'll be able to look past my hideous wealth and marry me after all?" David teased. "I can only promise you endless music, of course, so if there is another that can offer you more—"

But he was unable to continue as his future wife stopped his words with a passionate kiss.

"Oh David," Harmony said with a blushing yet bold look. "You can offer me far more than that."

About Emily E K Murdoch

If you love falling in love, then you've come to the right place.

I am a historian and writer and have a varied career to date: from examining medieval manuscripts to designing museum exhibitions, to working as a researcher for the BBC to working for the National Trust.

My books range from England 1050 to Texas 1848, and I can't wait for you to fall in love with my heroes and heroines!

Follow me on twitter and instagram @emilyekmurdoch, find me on facebook at facebook.com/theemilyekmurdoch, and read my blog at www.emilyekmurdoch.com.

www.ingramcontent.com/pod-product-compliance
Lightning Source LLC
Chambersburg PA
CBHW071944190726
48293CB00004B/1329